Twice Sharpened

Twice Sharpened

The Two-Edged Sword

Sequel to

Dark Stars of THE TWILIGHT

By

Marilyn Olson

authorHOUSE®

AuthorHouse™
1663 Liberty Drive
Bloomington, IN 47403
www.authorhouse.com
Phone: 1-800-839-8640

Dedication page illustration by Emily Eichinger
Illustrations by Elizabeth Berg

First published by AuthorHouse 09/26/2011

ISBN: 978-1-4670-3640-5 (sc)
ISBN: 978-1-4670-3641-2 (ebk)

Library of Congress Control Number: 2011916877

Printed in the United States of America

Thanks to:

My loving husband, children, grandchildren, friends, and the many cast and crew members of MCO Productions.

Dedication

To the One who gave everything so that we could be reunited with the Father.

Adventures in Heaven await us!

Table of Contents

Foreword

How well can we know the mind of Christ? As part of his body, can we understand his thoughts, his desires, or his motivations? Jesus' spoken words give us not only a clue as to his character, but as to the questions we all have about life on Earth: Why are we here? How did we get here? Why is it we can't remember anything before this span of time on Earth? What will we remember when the dark glass is taken away so that we can at last see TRUTH face to face?

Who are the "Sons of God?" Why does the Bible call us "Sons of God?" Who was Jesus before he was "begotten" of the Father?

Hidden within the pages of Scripture is a fascinating story. I have attempted to bring it to you through TWICE SHARPENED, The Two-Edged Sword.

This account is intended to inspire thought and research into the character of Jesus through the scriptures. Though the story is Biblically based, the connecting story line is fictional.

For an in-depth study, keep a Bible nearby to check references as you enjoy the book.

Marilyn Olson

For the word of God is quick, and powerful, and sharper than any two-edged sword.

Hebrew 4:12

Characters

Book 1
1. Korel (Karli)
2. Jano (Mattie, Karli's best frined)
3. Lusilite (Lucy, Karli's older sister)
4. Nagee (Korel's guardian angel)
5. Rutsch (Jano's guardian angel)
6. Jesus/Yeshua
7. Lucifer/Satan/Light
8. Karli's oldest sister ("Dawn" in book 3)

Book 2
1. Pinnac/Lusilite (Lucy, Karli's older sister)
2. Light (Lucifer/Satan)
3. Jucola, a Seraph—minor character in book 2
4. Korel (Karli)
5. Jano (Mattie)
6. Jeric (Pinnac's guardian angel)
7. Jesus/Yeshua
8. Suja (secondary character)
9. Emma (secondary character)
10. Ben (secondary character)

Book 3

1. Korel (Karli)
2. Jano (Mattie)
3. Pinnac/Lusilite (Lucy, Karli's older sister)
4. Jeric (Pinnac's guardian angel)
5. Jucola (a Seraph)
6. Nagee (Korel's guardian angel)
7. Rutsch (Jano's guardian angel)
8. Dawn (Karli's oldest sister)

Prologue

Out of his mouth went a sharp two-edged sword and his countenance was as the sun shining in his strength.

Rev 1:16

The Word, strong and powerful, could divide with its sharpness the thoughts of the mind from the intents of the heart. Sent to the world—a darkened place where good and evil existed together—the Word began the separation process.

Who would ultimately choose evil over good? Who, by contrast, were the enslaved sitting in darkness longing to be free?[1]

We were touched by the Bringer of Light. It was HE who brought the sword of the Word to Earth conquering evil with truth. He, who'd been with the Father since the beginning, was to live as mankind, bringing enlightenment of the Kingdom to Earth. The Kingdom of Heaven, once lost to us, could now be regained.

How had one-third of Heaven been banished from the heavenlies? Pride, arrogance and jealousy began growing within the heart of a much beloved archangel. Anti-God, anti-good, he became a black void growing in a perfect

---

[1]   Matt 4:16, Isaiah 61:1, 2 Tim 2:19

universe. His cancer of evil needed to be excised from the rest.

It was a process not only involving war of gigantic proportions, but also requiring sacrifice of a magnitude no one could have imagined. It's a story of light vs. darkness, truth vs. lies, hatred vs. love, and the powerful Word[2] of the Father being sent out to divide the evil from the good. It is the account of victory overcoming the wretchedness of evil, and restoration offered to all.

Where does one begin with a story that has no ending? To begin at the beginning is impossible, for there is also no beginning. With a point in time we will start, and fan out from there in this never-ending tale of eternity, love and forgiveness.

---

[2]   Names of God are capitalized. THE WORD, I AM, HEAVENLY FATHER, JEHOVAH, LORD, THE ALMIGHTY—though emphasizing different aspects of his character, all refer to the same Divine Being.

Chapter 1

The End of an Era

That search may be made in the book of the records . . .
Ezra 4:15

Korel[3] and Jano[4] exchanged glances. Best friends and closer than brothers, they needed no words to express what both of them at that moment now realized: the assignment was finished, the era of "mankind" was over, and from this instant their lives would change.

Joyful with the long awaited repentance and restoration of Pinnac,[5] Korel reverted to his childhood boyishness and playfully yelled to his friend, "Race you!"

Jano quickly accepted the challenge. They both took off running as fast as they could toward the housing complex where they'd lived for the last millennium.

Shouting and jumping as they raced across the field, they were giddy with the knowledge that their assignment for the past thousand years had been completed. All their efforts had

---

[3]   The story of Korel (Kor-EL') is told in the book <u>The Twinkling</u> © 2008 by Marilyn Olson.

[4]   Pronounced JAH'noh

[5]   Pinnac's (Pin-NAK') story can be found in <u>Dark Stars of the Twilight</u>, © 2009 by Marilyn Olson.

paid off; Earth was once more a heavenly paradise where HIS will was done as in Heaven. Millions of prayers had been answered, the lost were found, all things had been restored to the CREATOR OF ALL and Heaven was whole again. Only a very few in the outer edges of the universe were missing with names blotted out of the heavenly records of the Book of Life.

Reaching the complex together, Korel took the lead as he bounded up the steps two at a time.

"What's your hurry?" asked Jano, catching his breath.

"As if you didn't know," responded Korel. "Ziphotan, here I come!"

Jano knew about Korel's passion for his orchards located on Ziphotan. There he enjoyed experimenting with various fruits, developing new strains of apples and other exotic hybrids. It was a fervor created by the I AM Himself, and Korel was more than ready to return to his former life. "Ziphotan, here we come!" repeated Jano, with emphasis on the "we."

Korel paused a moment, pondering his friend. Jano had been there for him all through his difficult childhood on Earth and they'd been inseparable ever since. Being assigned to the same judicial seat for the great Day of Judgment had been a bonus. Together with Christ their team had determined the placement of countless individuals who'd not accepted the available gift of salvation while on Earth.[6] It had been a long and tedious job, with many procedures transpiring, but they'd completed their assigned tasks together.

Noticing a new message in their communication box, Jano stopped to open it.

"What is it?"

"The code to our next assignment." Punching the numbers into the tiny coding device on his wrist he soon discovered their immediate destination. "Looks like we're headed to Nexor."

---

[6]   We shall judge angels. 1 Cor 6:3

Korel broke into a wide grin. "Okay!" he responded, for Nexor was a vacation spot highly regarded for its many enjoyable and unique experiences.

"As former millennial judges, it's essential to take a time for rest and debriefing," Jano continued reading instructions from the decoding device. "After all your residual questions from the past era have been completely and satisfactorily answered, you may then continue the journey to the Third Heaven."

"So, we're headed to Nexor not only to revitalize our strength but to solve unanswered questions?" surmised Korel.

"Do you have questions?" responded Jano.

Silent for a moment in sudden serious contemplation, Korel shook his head. "No, I don't. Do you?"

"Yes, I have to say that I do," Jano quietly admitted.

"Then, Nexor, here we come!" Korel would accompany his friend; understanding the truth about puzzling situations was a vital and attainable element in Kingdom living.

Because the two friends had been busy up to the final days of the era, they were amongst the last to leave for this debriefing necessity. The stop at Nexor was apparently a prerequisite to attending the grand celebrations in the Third Heaven, a seasonal event all angels eagerly anticipated.

Quickly packing, the two friends soon headed toward a small intergalactic Skyper to embark for the trip.

As they entered the vehicle, they noticed a diminutive angel named Jeric running toward them. Usually happy and jovial, he appeared now to be in a somewhat somber mood. Nevertheless he stuck out his thumb in a jocular fashion, knowing full well his meaning would be instantly understood.

"You want to join us?" Jano yelled out of the cockpit.

"Beats using my wings. Where're you headed?"

"Nexor, then to the Third Heaven for the celebration."

"That's my destination as well."

"Okay. Hop in." Unknown to Korel, Jeric had just become aware that his earthly charge, Pinnac,[7] had in the end chosen evil over good and was now on the outskirts of the universe with the other enemies of the Kingdom.

Throwing his bag through the door, Jeric jumped into the Skyper. Though burdened with his undisclosed information, he nevertheless flashed one of his smiles, for he truly had a remarkably resilient personality.

---

[7]   Jeric had been Pinnac's guardian angel.

Nexor was located three galaxies away from the agricultural planet Ziphotan. Well known for its fun, parties, and delightful activities, this little planet was a popular vacation playground. Good restaurants, a buzzing city life, unusual entertainment and drinks of different flavors and textures were offered in abundance; it was an ideal choice of place to rest and be refreshed.

Arriving at the small planet they observed the milling crowds as they landed at the port.

"Didn't know there'd be so many here," noted Korel as they exited the vehicle.

Walking down the corridor to the terminal, they noticed a list of activities prominently placed by the walkway. "Hey, there's a three mile water slide nearby," noted the adventurous Jano. "Want to try it out?"

"I'm game—if you ride the zip lines with me," responded Korel, knowing the little child in him would be satiated by juvenile thrills within the hour.

Jeric, seeing some of his friends in the terminal, made plans for a later rendezvous with his traveling hosts and quickly bid them goodbye. Jano and Korel, after establishing the whereabouts of their rooms, grabbed their suits and headed to the water park.

The next hours were carefree as they hiked, boated, swam, and enjoyed playing the many sports offered at the compound. Rafting down the white water rapids, Jano and Korel rekindled their love for the simple pleasures of life.

It had been tough, evaluating their peers. Yet as judges they'd finished the task assigned to them while accepting the results as just. Some had not, in the end, accepted the free gift of salvation as was hoped. Though every opportunity had been given to those in question, their own personal choice of evil over good had made the final sad decision for them.

The proverbial sheep had been separated from the goats;[8] the wheat had been gathered and the tares had been destroyed.[9] It was finished, and the division was accomplished.

So be it.

After the hours of fun and frolic the two friends sat down at a well-known eatery famous for its unusual drinks. Observing their surroundings, they noticed the crowd: a boisterously happy group. There were many warrior angels, triumphant in battle, relating to each other the stories of war and victories of the last few millenniums. As expected, their unpredictable stories of temporary defeats all ultimately turned into triumphs for the Kingdom.

Standing quietly by the door was a tall seraph. Seraphim are identifiable due to their six wings and seemingly benign personalities. Created with numerous ways of seeing, they can take in their surroundings in an unassuming way without having much to say. Always content, these angels appear to blend into the background and are not much noticed.[10]

This particular seraph was vaguely familiar to Korel; he determined to know why before the evening was over. Mulling through his memory as to where he'd seen him, he was interrupted in his thoughts by a beautiful angel named Dawn.[11]

"Remember me?" Dawn squatted down beside the table, looking mischievously up into his face.

---

[8]   Matt 25: 32
[9]   See Matt 13: 25-40
[10]   Seraphim angels are defined with having six wings. Isa.6:2. For multiple internal eyes, see Rev 4:8
[11]   Karli's oldest sister of her two sisters on Earth. Though an eternal being, the feminine usage of pronouns is used to avoid confusion.

"How could I forget?" Korel brightened at the sight of her. Smiling, Korel acknowledged his acquaintance, having spent much of their earthly lives together in a deceptive situation. Happily, Dawn had discovered the truth about the lies she'd been told on Earth and had found closure regarding the chaos they'd caused.

"Would you care to join us?" asked Jano. "Sure." Dawn sat in the chair offered and looked contentedly at Korel for a moment before speaking.

"You weren't the person I thought you were," she remarked casually. "We were Kingdom sisters as well as earthly ones. I didn't realize it then, but now I do."

Taken aback, Korel only nodded, for he knew what Dawn was attempting to say. That Dawn had not understood the truth about Karli[12] during her lifetime on Earth didn't diminish the fact that now the truth was recognized. In the attempt to "correct" her, Dawn had abused Karli; she'd consistently believed their sister Lucy's lies against her. No apology was needed, but Korel was curious.

"Why now?"

"You were my unanswered question, the mystery I couldn't figure out. Why were you so successful when apparently you were so sinful? Now I know that I, not you, had been deceived.

"Lies permeated our existence on Earth," Jano interjected. We were all misled in one area or another. No one had perfect clarity on everything."

"When I understood the facts in light of truth, it brought tremendous healing," responded Korel.

"The heavenly record is accurate," Dawn continued. ". . . Just took me awhile to believe it."

"Thanks for letting me know." Korel smiled, as no more words were needed at the moment. As Dawn got up to rejoin her party, Korel softly sang "—one of the most beautiful people in the whole wide world," knowing Dawn was still within earshot. Turning back, Dawn bowed a curtsy along with an exaggerated swag of the hips in response.

Enjoying the banter, Jano hoped his unresolved issues would be clarified as thoroughly.

"Her issue was me," Korel turned to Jano. "What's yours?"

"Timmy Benito."[13]

"—one of the well-known tele-evangelists of the twenty-first century. I recall his programs."

---

[12]   Karli was Korel's earthly name.
[13]   Fictional name

"Timmy Benito spent his life preaching the gospel. His ministry seemed valid: he spoke to thousands, casting out devils in Jesus name, wrote books, and was interviewed many times by Christian media. Yet, the words he heard at Judgment were 'Depart from me; I never knew you.' On the other hand Mac Slater,[14] the sex offender, was welcomed into Heaven as a mighty man of God."

"I remember." As Korel relived the scene, he admitted there seemed to be a juxtaposition of the two cases. "I've pondered this myself, how what was seemingly accurate on Earth was so backwards at Judgment.

"So, that's my unanswered question."

"I see."

As they finished their drinks, Korel again noticed the seraph at the door. He once more tried to recall the circumstances but couldn't place him at all.

"Where have I seen him?" he muttered to himself, not really expecting Jano to know. As he again searched his memory, the tall seraph extracted himself from his surroundings and casually walked over to the table.

Too late. Jano was unable to remind Korel that seraphim were able to hear as well as see all that happened in the room.

"Jucola's[15] my name." The seraph spoke clearly—confidently—as if he was at their table by appointment. "You're right. You've seen me once before; it was during your Pit existence. Do you remember now?"

"Not really."

---

[14]   Fictional name
[15]   Pronounced Joo-COE-la

Though Korel had forgotten, seraphim forget nothing. For this reason, being good storytellers came naturally to them.

"It was in the deepest part . . . Do you want me to continue?"

Immediately captivated, Jano and Korel answered simultaneously, "Please do!"

Listening intently, the two friends were singularly attentive as Jucola told the most fascinating of stories.

Chapter 2
Jucola's Story

Above it stood the seraphim: each had six wings; the posts of the door moved . . .

Isa 6:2-4

Long ago within the massive hierarchy of Heaven the tiniest of details was nondescriptly put into place. A quiet seraph was commissioned as doorkeeper to the inner chambers of a well-beloved angel of Light. With not much to say and seemingly no opinions about anything, this tall seraph was perfect for the assignment, for truth be told, he really did not like to audibly chat.

One of the characteristics of this tranquil angel was that he had a memory that forgot nothing. He could remember days, events, times and places as well as every spoken word and gesture.

His name was Jucola, and he thoroughly enjoyed watching the brilliant angel named Light[16] conduct his many assignments.

Often Light created new instruments of worship within his inner chamber. These would be used to accompany choirs and other musical events as an integral part of

---

[16]   "Light" is Lucifer's nickname.

Heaven's joyful rallies. Dancing and singing praise to the ALMIGHTY of the Heaven of Heavens was an occurrence that never became routine.

Though Jucola said little, his inner life was rich with his work. He enjoyed seeing the implementations of new instruments as well as observing the interesting activity that took place in Light's presence.

As beings of great status were ushered into the inner chamber of this powerful angel, Jucola inwardly chronicled the events. His memory was always busy as he organized his thoughts. Joyful in his placement, he had no desire to change his position to anything other than what he was doing.

Jucola, however, kept a secret only he knew about. Though he obeyed every directional given to him, he was not technically under Light's authority. He'd never been, nor would he ever be under his control, for he was under the order of seraphim that answered only to the I AM.

Light eventually found much favor with the FATHER for his creative works of music. As the ages swept by, he was given more and more of Heaven's masses to oversee. Meeting these new challenges with capable wisdom, he flourished in his new status. Eventually joining the ranks of archangels Michael and Gabriel, he, along with other sons of God, could regularly be in the presence of the I AM.[17]

The fact he was found worthy by the Highest was an immeasurable achievement. Beautifully developing his gift of music, he repeatedly brought the masses of choirs

---

[17] See Job 1:6 for Satan's access to the Lord and the sons of God. This access was apparently still allowed even after his rebellion and subsequent fall.

to roaring praise of adulation to the epitome of love, God Himself.

Returning home, jubilant after his first extended visit in the Highest Heaven with the sons of God, Light happily embraced all who came his way. Joyfully he sang and shouted as he danced down the street to his bright residence, for he'd sought long and hard to perfectly impress his Creator, and had succeeded.

"Congratulations!" he heard the pleasant voice. Greeting him was Jucola, the little noticed seraph who rarely caught his attention. Without a word, Light grabbed his hands and spun him around in a dance.

Amused, Jucola was more than a bit surprised with the spur-of-the-moment merriment; he laughed good-naturedly as he righted his six wings. Folding each one carefully, he meticulously tucked them back into place.

"It's not every day I get a 'congratulations' from a seraph," Light exclaimed. Jucola nodded a happy acknowledgment of his pleasantries.

Because seraphim angels have the ability to stand motionless at their post for an indefinite length of time, they easily blend into their surroundings. Consequently, Light didn't usually notice his doorkeeper.

The irony of his position was not lost on him, however, for though seraphim seem above rank to the general angel population none had ever attained the rank of archangel. Light was understandably ecstatic with the fact that he himself had attained it.

For numerous millenniums to follow the archangel Light served with rigor the I AM. With singleness of purpose he taught all those under his authority to do the same.

As he increased in ability and power, more and more angels were given into his care. His numbers of angels grew until fully one-third of Heaven was under his management.

Life was good. The unpredictable became the predictable, for Light was constantly able to put his creative gifts to use in structuring and delivering new forms of worship, music and praise. For millions and millions of eternities life existed in this pleasant and active state.

During this pre-world existence many subtle changes took place. Now, even as unfamiliar routines began to unfold before him, Jucola still kept an accurate account of every guest that came through Light's door. His position made him privy to details no one else knew; he could not only remember each visitor by name, but could also repeat word for word every conversation uttered in his presence. Jucola had been placed there by the Great I AM, but for reasons no one else remembered nor could have foreseen.

As the ages passed into immeasurable lengths, the mood of the placement continued to gradually change. Intermittently, Jucola would catch a glimpse of Light's distant look—one that both haunted and unnerved him.

These occasional looks, he surmised, were not ones of contentment, but rather longings for something else. Though he'd achieved the highest rank possible to an angel, Light appeared to want more status.

Jucola, quiet as a mouse and just as much noticed was inadvertently privy to the start of Light's deteriorating thoughts: *Who is higher in rank than I? No one! I must be regarded by my subordinates to be equal to the I AM. I must learn the power of THE WORD and use it to my advantage.*

The Word. This was where all power originated. Light longed to be able to speak so that the spoken became fact.

He often daydreamed: *to have the kind of eternal, creative power that the I AM has . . . to speak the Word and the Word creates existence.*[18] This thought grew until it consumed his every thought.

Soon the discontent in his thoughts seeped into his being. He dreamed of creating a new order, one where he'd reign supreme. Desiring to equate himself with God, he came up with a startling idea. Developing it, he schemed a plan to replace the supremacy of the I AM.

Opposites! A new creation with everything the opposite of good. The night of this discovery was for him a tremendous breakthrough. Much like a black hole is a negative to the movement in the universe, his creation would be a negative to the creation of good.

The Father is 'love' so I'll be defined as 'hate.' The Father is truth, I'll be lies. He created life, therefore I'll create death. As he formulated his sinister plan, he chose a name for his new creation: "Evil." *Evil will replace the Father's creation of "good."* Excited about his unique conception, Lucifer[19] carefully schemed how to implement it into law.

Heaven is an orderly place where authority and chain of command is highly structured. Lucifer knew the Father would never break his own laws, so he worked within the premise of that organization; he used his authority to teach his subordinates his new way. Evil, he surmised, was stronger than good, and with that presupposition, Lucifer determined to make himself the sole ruler of his new world.

He began the process by placing restrictive orders within the top echelons of the ranks under him, then letting those

---

[18]   John 1:1-3
[19]   "Light" will now be identified by his real name, "Lucifer."

restrictions filter down to the rest. Next he sent out special invitations to some of the top leaders, as well as to those not so well known in his domain. Most were clueless as to what was happening.

Jucola's position was such that only through his door could the invited guests enter into the inner rooms of Lucifer's quarters. He could see that those summoned were not only loyal, but also naive as to Lucifer's true motivations. He also realized that his status made him unique among the personages of the conference that was taking place just under his nose. That he was basically overlooked was a design of his position implemented ages ago, long before any thought of insurrection had entered the realms of heavenly perfection. Now he realized that in the Father's wisdom he had set the boundaries in place if ever such a situation should arise.

He had seen much.

Chapter 3

The Truth Leaks Out

—Bring them that sit in darkness out of prison.

Isa 42:7

The time had come once again for Jucola's seasonal visit to the highest heaven. With no fanfare and not a shrug of a change from the routine, he entered his personal Skyper and left for the journey. Within his memory were the names of all those involved in the treachery.

He mentally prepared what he would say: "Lucifer, entrusted with the well-being of masses of angels, has grown increasingly envious of the I AM'S power and dominion. He's created an evil force and has enacted laws restricting true worship of the Father for all under his authority."

Entering the highest heaven he quickly transported to the throne room where Michael, Gabriel, and twenty-four elders were gathered. Bowing deeply before the I AM, he realized no words were needed, for HE was instantly aware of the subversion. The loving eyes of the Father were filled with grief for those locked under this evil scheme.

Michael spoke up. "The question now is how to restore the ones affected." The fact that so much authority had been given to Lucifer made this an extremely complex situation.

Obviously, the I AM was not short on ultimate wisdom and power. His creation of good would defeat evil once and for all. However the victory would not come without a price.

Michael quickly put the battle strategy into place. Jucola must return to his post in order to convey all pertinent information to Michael. The news of the insurrection would be kept quiet for now.

"Here, take this." Michael handed Jucola a small round instrument. "You can download your information to this device simply through the flicker of your eye. Jucola looked at the small device. Round, magnetic, and not much bigger than a small coin, he surmised correctly that he could keep it hidden in his Skyper: it perfectly matched the other dials located on the dash. Even if found it would be useless without the code. Additionally, it was designed to function only with the unique twinkle of his own eye. It's true use would never be discovered.

"Be alert, Jucola" Michael warned as Jucola headed back to his Skyper. "Lucifer's power should not be underestimated."[20]

Knowing his placement was important in obtaining accurate information for the battle ahead, Jucola once more headed back to Nexor.

Nearing the port of entry he was unexpectedly surrounded by Lucifer's elite. *This is unusual. Do they already know my true mission?* As he exited the Skyper, he was escorted back to his post by two of them.

"What's happening?" he asked.

"New regulation. Everyone who enters here must now be cleared."

---

[20] Jude 1:9 The archangel Michael, during a dispute with Lucifer (Satan), didn't dare accuse him, but said "The Lord rebuke you."

After a thorough search of his person, Jucola was allowed to return to his position by the door—his true assignment hadn't been discovered. Though outwardly appearing benign, inwardly he'd become increasingly wary. *I must gather information while I can.*

One day a little-known angel named Pinnac excitedly walked through the door. As was customary, Jucola silently led him to the inner chamber; he dared not speak a word of warning. Motionless, he documented all that transpired between them.

Soon after Pinnac's visit, the top echelons of Lucifer's new power elite met to finalize the plans for the takeover rally. The time was set to coincide with the seasonal worship in the Third Heaven; no one would be allowed to leave the planet. For the first time in history one-third of the angels would be absent. All under Lucifer's dominion would be required to stay here and worship only him.

This is it! I must leave while I still can. Finding an opportune time when no visitors were coming or leaving, Jucola quietly exited the structure and cautiously returned to his Skyper. The information he had was vital; he needed to get it to Michael as soon as possible.

Entering the cockpit, he quickly downloaded the information into the small storage device located by the dials. This was not hard—all he had to do was stare at the device for a moment in concentration. With just a twinkle of his eye all stored information in his memory became imprinted on the core of the tiny unit. As he punched in the needed code, he knew this vital information was safe and could now only be accessed by the warrior angel Michael.

No sooner had he done this than his Skyper was surrounded by Lucifer's newly commissioned thugs.

"Treason," they snarled as they commandeered his ship.

Unwittingly, Jucola had become Lucifer's first prisoner of war—not because his true loyalties had been discovered, however. It was because of another reason altogether: his was the only working Skyper on the planet.

Because Skypers were programmed, maintained and controlled with the technology from the "good" side, the dark forces hadn't foreseen that their vehicles could so easily be rendered useless. All Skypers used by Lucifer's subordinates had been de-programmed.

It was unknown to Lucifer's cohorts why Jucola's Skyper hadn't been affected, but it was quickly commandeered for Lucifer's personal use.

Soon war of gigantic proportions broke out in the heavenlies. Lucifer and those under him were quickly banished from Heaven and fell to Earth; a huge barrier swept across the heavenlies to block any attempted re-entry. Eventually the core of the earth became their prison.[21]

Meanwhile, Jucola as a prisoner of war was bound and taken to the deepest parts of the Pit. Shackled to the walls for an eternity, he soon lapsed into a state of suspended animation. He wouldn't be released until rescued by the Liberator from Heaven.

Jucola sat down. The room was packed with listeners, all intently focused on the story.

"What happened?"

"Simple. I didn't move until I heard the words "It is finished." The spoken WORD released me, along with all other POW's."

---

[21]   See Job 33: 24-30; also the story is told in detail in <u>Dark Stars of The Twilight,</u> copyright 2009 by Marilyn Olson.

THE WORD.

The seraph quietly stood up, signaling the story was over. As the guests clapped in appreciation, he returned to his post beside the door.

So, Jucola had been a prisoner in the recesses of the Pit. Korel correctly deduced that this is where he had seen the angel: he'd been shackled to the wall as a prisoner of war.[22]

Fascinated with the story, the two friends bid goodnight to the dwindling crowd and made their way to their quarters for some much needed sleep.

---

[22]   For more of this story, read <u>THE TWINKLING</u> by Marilyn Olson, © 2008.

Chapter 4
An Archive Visit

There is joy in the presence of the angels of God over one sinner that repents.

Luke 15:10

Though the present was so magnificent in comparison, the Father knew that truth was the best antidote to the residual lies that were still causing unanswered questions. Some of the redeemed needed nurturing as they readjusted to a world where only truth was told. Others were still babies, indeed, having been "born again" into the Kingdom, but having grown very little because of one reason or another.[23]

Archive stations were accessible for the Redeemed on numerous planets throughout the universe. These had been set up for purposes of clarifying puzzling issues regarding experiences on Earth. Those of mankind who'd grieved missing loved ones and had come to Heaven with some misunderstandings as to their real nature could find closure

---

[23] A comparison would be a loving mother who cares for a small baby, teaching it only the things he can handle at each maturity level. See 1 Cor 3:2; Heb 5:12-13; 1 Peter 2:2

in these stations. Truth not only brought understanding of confusing events, but healing of them as well.

Most of the Redeemed had by now taken advantage of this service. Because Jano had been busy up until the last days of Judgment, however, he'd not yet had the opportunity. Jano's unanswered questions about the judging process needed to be resolved.

Why was Timmy Benito rejected and Mac Slater honored?

The next morning before they met up with Jeric, Korel and Jano visited a branch of the archives located nearby. Entering the large building, Korel punched in the code for the twenty-first century. Sitting in the comfortable chairs as the screen came to life, they watched the lives of the ones in question play out.

In looking at the archive analyzer it soon became apparent that the "facts" on Earth did not meet the standard of truth in Heaven. The "sex offender" had been falsely accused by an underage and very immoral foster sister. She accused him in order to hide her promiscuous past.

Eighteen-year-old Mac had been taken in for questioning, lied to and threatened. He was questioned hours upon hours without sleep; the interrogators were convinced of his guilt because of the details provided by the foster child.

Having been home-schooled and protected, Mac was no match for the manipulations of this experienced force. He believed them when they told him he'd failed a lie detector test and would absolutely be convicted as a sexual predator. They continued the interrogation with threats that once he was in prison, he'd be repeatedly raped unless he became a "wife" and therefore protected by his convict "husband."

Mac had been so scared that his first sexual experience would be a prison initiated homosexual rape that he accepted the untrue plea bargain rather than take a chance on losing in court. Innocent, he was scared into falsely admitting guilt and accepted the lifelong label of a sex offender.[24]

His life changed forever. Now he couldn't associate with anyone under the age of eighteen, including his own siblings. His probation requirements stipulated he pay for monthly lie detector tests. No longer could he pursue a career in teaching, but had to look for work wherever he could with the restrictions he had. His earthly jobs consisted of pumping gas and doing yard work.

As Mac got older, he attempted to recant his signed statement, but it was no use. His accuser, even as an adult, never found the courage to admit the truth to the authorities. Ultimately, Mac lived with the sex offender label and its restrictions for the rest of his life.

The evangelist, on the other hand, had been a deceiver of many. Greed had been his motivation for preaching.[25] He'd stolen intellectual material sent to him by the trusting and published it as if he had written it himself. His motivations for everything he did were self-exaltation, pride, money, and a quest for power and fame. He was, in reality, a wolf in sheep's clothing[26] that preyed upon the innocent, trusting and gullible. He masked his true goal with a fake humility while perpetuating a fraud upon God's people.

At Judgment he thought he could also fool God. "I've preached in your name, I've cast out devils."

"You've devoured widow's houses. You've stolen from my true servants. Depart from me. I never knew you."[27]

---

[24]   Based on an actual case
[25]   2 Cor. 11:13-14
[26]   Matthew 7:15
[27]   Mark 12:39-40. See also Matthew 7:22-23

By contrast, Mac Slater had grown spiritually strong as the years went by. He was able to forgive those who'd lied and manipulated him into this situation. He prayed often for those who had treated him unjustly. As a result, he was able to genuinely minister to others who found themselves in similar circumstances. His advice and comfort, birthed from walking through the proverbial fire was accepted and received by the hurting. His ministry was strong as he helped many to find the answers they needed to thrive in the Kingdom.

Faithful to God in life, he was rewarded upon death with the words "Well done, good and faithful servant. Enter into the joy of the Lord."[28]

Upon this revelation, Jano's questions were answered to his complete satisfaction.

Anxious to get started to the Third Heaven, the two friends reconnected with Jeric, who by this time was looking much more rested and refreshed.

"All set to go?" Korel beamed to his friend.

"Absolutely." Jeric flashed his infectious grin. The three headed to the Sky Port, entered the Skyper, and punched in the code for the journey.

---

[28] See Matt 25.21-46

Chapter 5
On to the Third Heaven

[one was} caught up to the Third Heaven

2 Cor. 12:2

The Third Heaven was the place where, before the rapture, the Redeemed of Earth found themselves after death. A beautiful, welcoming city, each of the Redeemed had arrived with personal guardian angels to help them re-adjust to life.

"The beautiful streets of gold . . . I want to walk on them again," declared Jano enthusiastically.

"Righto," Korel responded with a happy twinkle in his eye, also re-living the experience. The unusual pavement, luminous in its golden hue, had caressed his feet as he walked on its sparkling surface. The buildings were also unique, giving musical sounds which blended together into a pleasant symphony as he walked with his own guardian angel, Nagee.[29]

These memories sparked in Korel an interest as well to return to that beautiful place. *My trip to Ziphotan can wait.*

"How was your visit to Nexor?" Jeric, ever the bright optimist, casually asked after takeoff.

---

[29] Pronounced Na-GEE" with a hard G.

"Illuminating," Jano answered in a word.

"Questions answered?"

"Absolutely. I'm glad we took the detour."

"I've also a question."

Surprised, Jano turned to face Jeric.

"You? I thought guardian angels have no need for clarification of earthly events."

"Usually, no. However, one thing has me puzzled." Getting the attention of both Jano and Korel, Jeric continued. "I'd like to visit the archives to see if I can discover the answer."

It didn't occur to Korel that any of the guardian angels would want to see the archives. *Hadn't they already had access to the events on Earth? Didn't they automatically understand the facts surrounding each mortal? What information could he possibly lack? He didn't experience a sin nature or exist in a clouded state of reality like we did."* As he mulled over these thoughts, Jeric came out with a startling statement.

"I want to understand the mind of Christ. How is it he alone volunteered to defeat Lucifer on his own turf while none of the rest of us dared?"

It was an astonishing question. To know the mind of Christ . . . this particular thought had never crossed Jano's mind.

"Do we have the right to know?" questioned Korel. "Would his life even be in the archives at any rate? The archives were set up for all who'd been on Earth during the long war, but does that include giving us access to the inner thoughts of Jesus?"

"The fact that he lived on Earth as 'mankind' might qualify his life as accessible," interjected Jano.[30]

---

[30]   See Ps 90:8 and Jeremiah 23:24

"I guess there's one way to find out."

Intrigued, even Korel, who'd earlier felt he had no need for an archive visit, was interested. Though longing to return to his precious orchards on Ziphotan, his curiosity was again piqued with something of much more interest.

"I'm game," he stated enthusiastically. How about you?"

"Sure!" Jano was just as eager to explore the possibilities.

Jeric's desire to understand the inner thoughts of Jesus brought about another change of plans for the trio. The fact that Korel and Jano would accompany him would be his delight; for though his assigned Pinnac hadn't accepted salvation, he'd been able to rejoice in Korel and Jano's changed lives.[31] Their recent experiences together had deepened their friendship more than throughout the whole of eternity before the "fall."[32]

"The archives are available numerous places, but since we're headed to the Third Heaven we should watch them there. You ought to see the building!" The memories of the place suddenly overwhelmed Korel's emotions. "Do you remember the city, Jano?"

"Remember?" Of course! It was right before the Rapture! How could I ever forget?" Indeed, it had preceded one of the greatest highlights of his existence.

The Rapture!

Abruptly the conversation turned to this event. Also known as the "great catching up of believers" the experience had been so astonishing that it clearly left a deep imprint. The antithesis of the "Fall," the catching up had been as

---

[31]   Luke 15:10. The angels rejoice when sinners repent.

[32]   "Fall" refers to Lucifer's fall, not Adam's. See Isa 14:12

joyful as the casting out had been sorrowful. It continued to be a popular topic of discussion among the redeemed.

"Caught up together with Christ our Lord!" Jano sing-songed as they traveled through the galaxies. Jesus was an incredible hero to the rest of the "sons of God," as the Redeemed were now also known. Korel and Jeric joined in the song as they entered the heavenly city's atmosphere and prepared to disembark.

Not knowing how long the archives would be available, the travelers decided to make visiting them a priority.

Korel, however, first wanted to look up his old friend Nagee. Perhaps he'd join them. Opening a small directory he found the needed code and quickly informed Nagee of his location. Of course, Jano notified Rutsch[33] that they'd arrived. It had been over a thousand years since either of them had seen their earthly guardian angels and they looked forward to the reunion with great anticipation.

Exiting the Skyper the friends soon arrived at the massive archive building.

The structure was unusual, with siding the consistency of sky and the color of a sunset. Surrounding it was an aura of light, fantastic in its color, deep in its hues, and intricately beautiful.

Approaching the building was like walking into a rainbow. Upon entering the sphere of the structure, the lights would warm them, then cool dramatically, teasing them with their sensations and smells. There was nothing on Earth that could compare with the experience.

Jeric was most eager for this event. Though he'd not experienced life as mankind he was, none-the-less, very eager to learn the answer to his question. To be privy to the

---

[33]   Jano's guardian angel on Earth. Pronounced Roo-CHAY'

private thoughts, motivations and workings of such a great mind as Christ's . . . what an adventure this would be!

"Got your message;" a voice halted the procession. It was Nagee and with him was Rutsch.

"Hey!" No sooner had the greeting been given but the friends were slapping each other on the shoulder in jubilant welcome.

"Long time no see," chuckled Nagee. Where've you been hiding yourself?"

"Earth. Just finished an assignment in the Day of Judgment for the Thousand Year Reign. How about you?"

"Working in Ziphotan."

Korel felt a momentary pang of homesickness. In this breadbasket region of the heavenlies, he liked nothing better than to experiment with new varieties of fruit. It had been a long time since he'd been home; however, the excitement of this present adventure more than made up for the delay of his return.

The small band of friends soon arrived at the door of the archives. Entering, they stopped in the lobby to look at the directory. There were many possible destinations. Jeric read from the list: "Creation, Adam, lineage of Abraham, David . . ."

Contemplating the numerous routes, Jano spoke, "Shall we start at zero BC?"

"No, back it up more."

"To where?"

"How about the beginning? 'In the beginning was the Word; the Word was with God and the Word was God.'"[34] Korel, quoting scripture, had a point, for they all knew the "beginning" for this eternity would include the fall of Lucifer.

---

[34]   John 1:1

"Okay." Jano typed WORD and turned the coordinates to the "beginning." Immediately the directory filled with endless possibilities covering an infinite amount of history. They'd be in the archives forever if the spectrum wasn't narrowed down. "We need to provide a specific point in time. Any suggestions?"

Korel immediately recalled Jucola's story. "How about starting at the point where Jucola sent the information to Michael?"

"Good idea." Punching in a few pertinent facts provided by the seraph's recent narrative, the friends soon found the exact place to start.

As Jano pressed the slight protrusion in the directory the floor began to gently move under them. Chairs appeared, forming a comfortable seating arrangement; sitting down they watched as the presentation begin. Shown in 360-degree surround mode, the room was soon filled with the most beautiful story of all time.

Chapter 6
A Point in Time

The worlds were framed by the Word of God.

Heb 11:3

He stretches out the north over the empty place and hangs the earth upon nothing.

Job 26:7

After receiving the vital information from Jucola, Michael called his warrior angels to the battle and filled them in on the recent events. "One-third are lost, clueless as to the truth of what's going on. By the time they realize they've been deceived, they'll be addicted to the power of evil.[35] Our strategy must be implemented carefully. Anything less than victory on all fronts is not an option."

Watching from the archives, the small group of friends once again witnessed the defeat and casting out of Lucifer and all those under him. It was a war of monumental proportions. Soon the barrier to Heaven stretched across the Universe; the quarantine of the cancer was thorough.

---

[35] For deceived, see 2 Tim 3:13, Job 12:16, Deut 11:16, Titus 3:3, Rev 19:20, Rev 20:10. For yoke of bondage, see Gal. 5:1

Observing the details of their harrowing deception and banishment brought a sense of sadness to the group. Lucifer, along with all those under his authority, now existed in the Pit of the earth.[36] Sitting in darkness, there were those who wouldn't have fallen had it not been for his calculated lies and manipulations.

We were slaves without hope.[37]

The scene moved to the private throne room where THE FATHER and THE WORD were formulating their plans. "We must bring them into the light—let them know the Kingdom of God is once again within reach. Seven days[38] will be the test. 'Mankind' will be the name of the newly created being that can house an eternal spirit.

"As humans they must each be given a chance—outside of Lucifer's total dictatorship—to choose whether to serve good or evil. In order for the choice to be accurate, all memories of former existence will be isolated into the subconscious recess of each memory."

"As long as they live as mortals they'll remember nothing. Faint traces of former memories could possibly make an appearance through dreams and occasional flashbacks, but there should be an atmosphere of safety within the families of man."

"Mothers will be created with a maternal impulse that is sacrificial in nature. Fathers will feel protective toward their wives and children. These natural instincts will balance out the evil that's dominated them for so long."

"Those with abusive parents?"

---

[36] See Psalms 88:6, Isa 14:15
[37] Psa 107:10, 1 Thes 4:13
[38] A day is as a thousand years in Heaven. 2 Peter 3:8

"They won't be deserted. I'll bring others who care into their lives—even affectionate pets—to teach them about goodness and love. All must be given a chance to choose their destiny. The TWO-EDGED SWORD can divide the intents from the thoughts; quick and powerful, the Word will know who longs to be with us, and who yearns for the Kingdom of Evil. At the end of the test we'll welcome our citizens home with immense joy."

"The pull of evil is devious as well as strong. Deception is a very real possibility, even for humans created without sin."

"I have a back-up plan, but I hope I don't have to use it."

"Let's begin." These simple words, spoken so quietly, were a gentle contrast to the dramatic events that would soon take place. The WORD was all that was needed to start the redemption process.

The sons gathered to begin the work. Earth, now without form and empty, was to be renovated.[39] A sun, moon, and stars would be created to light up the planet. The mission of bringing home the lost had begun.

LET THERE BE LIGHT![40]

---

[39]   Isa 14:17 Indicates that Lucifer not only made the world a wilderness and destroyed cities, but also kept prisoners.

[40]   Gen 1:3

Chapter 7

The Beginning

In the beginning was the Word and the Word was with God and the Word was God.

John 1:1

It was a joyful bunch, these sons of God. Getting together to decide which planets and galaxies would light up the nighttime of Earth, they shouted for joy when the morning stars sang together.[41] This glorious creation was pronounced "good"—a fine contrast to the evil that had once invaded the heavenlies.

The visible heavens were lighted. *Now to renovate the earth.*

THE WORD planned together with I AM the designs for the project. Together, they placed the sun for upper daytime lighting; they added vegetation, fish, birds, and animals to adorn and beautify the surface of Earth. Not only were the orbits engineered for the galaxies, but also the trajectories of the protons and neutrons were set in motion. Setting up the precise DNA links to be utilized in repopulating the earth, they put into motion the unique data needed for all living cells to divide and multiply.

---

[41]   Job 38:7

All things were formed; nothing created itself. Every element was generated fully through careful planning by the Father and the Word; without the Word, nothing was made.[42]

Soon their planning included concepts for the training of mankind.

"We must teach them to do what's good."

"We'll start with the basics, for they've been so long ingrained in the practices of darkness that they no longer remember how to live in the light."

"They're coming into the world free from all earlier influences and previous addictions. They'll now have freedom of choice to find the path leading to the Kingdom of God."

"We'll make it simple for them. For starters, the first human could get by with just one rule."

"Which is—"

"—don't eat from the Togae tree."

"Togae . . . the flowered tree in the center of the garden with the appealing, pleasant-smelling fruit—"

"—the Tree of Good and Evil. Obedience to this mandate will be the one and only law."

"Perfect. Now, who should be the first to experience being a human?"

"Let's start with Adam."

"Agreed. So be it."

Adam was a good choice. He'd once been a powerfully righteous being; yet caught under the authority of Lucifer he had no choice but to submit to the regime placed over him.[43] He was a suitable pick to father the races of Earth.

---

[42] John 1:3

[43] See 2 Tim. 1:9, 1 Cor 2:7, Titus 1:2, John 17:16, Eph 1:4,10

Once born into the world as mankind, Adam would be free from the domination of the evil one. By obeying the rules he could choose, rather, to serve the God of goodness. Those subsequently born from his seed would have his perfect adherence to the rules implanted in their inherited DNA, making it easier as time went by for those generations to make good decisions. He was the right selection to become the first human being on Earth.

Soon I AM created a body from the elemental dust of the earth. He formed it using his own image as the model.[44]

It's perfect.

Admiring his work, HE breathed into the mouth. As the lungs expanded with air, the heart began pumping and all the cells filled with oxygen. God's breath gave the body a living soul. Adam's spirit, snatched from the tunnel, completed the process.

Welcome, son Adam![45]

Adam had a swarthy physical appearance along with a gently strong face. Created with a conscience, he possessed a healthy sense of right versus wrong.

During the daytime Adam worked hard to name all the animals, a job his Creator had given him. It was fun to watch each species for characteristics that would spark a name. He learned which animals made good companions, which ones he could ride and which ones he could train.

Adam also enjoyed exploring the many caves and secret hideouts in the garden, often playing a game of hide and seek with his animal companions. But his favorite activity was to smell and taste all the interesting food from the fruit trees and numerous plants. Crushing some types of produce

---

[44] Mankind was made in the image of God. Gen 1:27; 9:6
[45] Adam was a son of God. Luke 3:38

to make oils and juices, grinding others for flours and experimenting with different combinations of ingredients was a delight of which he never got tired. Life was not dull in the garden!

Interacting with the animals was certainly interesting. He continually worked to discover what each was capable of doing—teaching new tricks to some while harnessing and utilizing the strength of others. Given the job of caring for the garden as well as naming the animals, his life on Earth was busy and rich with wonder.

Each evening the I AM would meet with Adam to discuss his day. These times of debriefing and fellowship were great enjoyment for both of them.

It wasn't long, however, until Adam noticed something amiss: each of the creatures in the garden had a special mate. He had none. Howbeit, in earth years he was still very young. God in His wisdom let him finish out his youth before moving to a more mature level.

One evening after their walk together through the garden, Adam heard the pleasant words, "I have a surprise for you."

"What is it?"

"You'll find out tomorrow."

That night Adam was awake a bit longer than normal, pondering the mystery of the secret surprise. *What can it be?* He'd been given many surprises since the beginning, the last being a little puppy that was the delight of his life. *Maybe a new species of animal to discover and name?*

Still excited, Adam suddenly fell into a deep, God-induced sleep.

Upon waking the next morning, still groggy and experiencing a slight twinge from a recent surgical removal of one of his ribs, he saw sleeping quietly beside him a beautiful human, not unlike himself, but yes, quite different.

Being logical in his thinking as well as intelligent, he soon put the pieces together as to whom she belonged and why she was there. Staring at the sleeping beauty beside him he thought long and hard about what name to call her. He finally settled upon the name "Eve." She would be the mother of all their descendants.

Eve, child-like and a bit naïve, had a personality opposite from the insuppressible Adam. She liked flowers and shiny, pretty things. She cared about how her hair looked each day. She also liked to decorate, and had a nesting instinct.

Adam watched in admiration as she organized an area under the trees into a comfortable and secluded home for their use. He had, up to this time, been satisfied with sleeping wherever he happened to lie down at night.

As he learned to please and care for his wife, he also learned how to value her differences from his own. He realized she relied on his strength, his wisdom and his leadership.

Now each evening both would enjoy the fellowship of their Heavenly Father. Shortly before the meetings, Eve would occasionally pick a flower to put into her long golden hair "for the occasion." Adam marveled at her feminine difference; he loved her with all his heart. Together, they learned to subdue the fast-growing foliage, making beautiful and intricate gardens out of the abundant plant life.

Though enjoying each other's company in the garden, there was still inborn within their spirits a dormant memory of their pre-earth state. Occasionally a nightmare would awaken one of them out of sleep. Yet, how wonderful to wake up after a bad dream to find themselves in this beautiful tropical garden, with temperature just right and nothing to cause pain.

As the young couple's days unfolded in joyful contentment, the unseen hosts of Heaven watched. The question remained unanswered: could they live without sin? The Togae tree was prominently placed. The one rule regarding it had been given: DO NOT EAT FROM ITS FRUIT. So far, Adam and Eve had easily obeyed this directive.

Though the tempter was aware of the test, he'd not yet made himself known to either Adam or Eve. His immediate goal was to encourage just one sin. This would get him a foothold in the world and with that foothold he could eventually regain total control.

The wily Satan wanted to thoroughly understand Eve's personality before he made his move. The hope in the heavenlies, of course, was that mankind's choices would always be made correctly, preventing sin and its addictions from entering the world.

As time progressed, the Togae tree, right in the center of the garden, was continually enticing the feminine Eve with its smell and tasty-looking fruit. It wasn't that she was hungry or bored with the other edible delights of the garden; simple curiosity drew her to it. Nevertheless, she obeyed the mandate, suppressing her desire to taste its fruit.

Besides, there are so many other types of fruits to taste and enjoy. I can even eat the delicious fruit from the Tree of Life, so I don't need to taste this one. She often stood by the tree observing its flowers and unique shapes. *There is, after all, no rule about just looking at it.*

Walking by the Togae tree one day she heard a voice she'd not heard before. The tone was silky smooth and surprisingly exciting.

"Did God absolutely say not to eat the fruit?" Hearing another entity was not really startling to Eve. She'd experienced continuous surprises since the day she woke up beside Adam.

Curious, she searched to find the source of the sound. Peering as close as she dared into the tree—for to even touch the tree was forbidden—she saw a beautiful, shiny serpent.

"Yes," she replied honestly. "We're not to eat it, or we'll die." *Interesting. Adam will be surprised to know there's a strikingly beautiful creature in the garden that can communicate verbally with us.* Conversing with the creature did seem a bit weird to Eve . . . she'd never seen a talking snake before. Her conversations up to this point had been limited to Adam and THE FATHER, so it was fascinating to get another view on things. In addition, the serpent's attractiveness increased the believability of his words.

"You won't die," the snake spoke confidently. "This is what you don't know. Once you eat this fruit, you'll become as gods, knowing good and evil. You want that, don't you? Eating the fruit will give you a shortcut to getting back to where you were before this current limited existence."

Shortcut? Eve's curiosity was piqued. *My mind will be open, able to understand our past as well as the details of why we're here.*

"Yes. As gods," he repeated. "This fruit is designed for eating; don't you see? Otherwise, why would it look so appetizing? Besides, *HE* knows its effect will give you insight into the spirit world you don't presently have. Taste it. You'll see I'm right."

The serpent, artfully expressive, spoke with exceptional eloquence. Lustrous and shiny, he was easily the most stunning creature in the garden. Eve, in awe of its charms, became convinced that his assertions were true.

So there is actually no danger at all? We can access superhuman capabilities?

She reached up to grab a ripe piece of fruit. It picked easily. Turning it around in her hands for a few minutes, she bent down to smell its aroma.

This smells wonderful!

At last she took a bite. Nothing much happened, although she did feel a small rush of excitement. *This feeling is pleasant.* Unknown to her, the dormant addiction of doing a prohibited act instantly grabbed hold and attached itself to her spirit; into her memory triggered the latent addictions of evil. It felt pleasurable for only a moment, but that was enough.

Not wanting to be alone in her discovery, she picked some more fruit and took it to Adam. *At this moment, according to the serpent, I'm more knowledgeable than he is. He's got to see that there's nothing wrong with eating this.* She picked a flower for her hair and put on her most pleasing smile.

"Here," she said sweetly. "Eat this. I did and see? Nothing bad happened. It's got an interesting taste I think you'll like."

Adam was adamantly opposed to eating the fruit; every fiber of his being cried out against this disobedient act. But Eve was holding it right in front of him and nothing appeared changed. She obviously had not died, as was the warning. *Yes, even to touch the tree is forbidden, yet here she is holding the fruit with a smile on her face.*

However, Adam was not fooled.[46] He had other thoughts. To leave Eve as a reprobate by herself was unthinkable to him. She was naïve, not understanding the unending

---

[46]   I Tim. 2:14

ramifications of her act. He knew she had a tendency to be more vulnerable than he.

How can I abandon the love of my life? What will happen to her? He couldn't bare the thought of separation from her. Though his conscience forbade him, his instincts told him to stay with her in order to protect her. If Eve was to die, then he was determined to die with her.

In his thoughts, though, Adam was truly deceived, for he instinctively felt the need to protect Eve from herself. Yet, in this line of thought he placed himself above the mandates of God, not trusting the outcome for her without him. Adam's protective feel towards Eve was God-given, yet now it was displaced. *Do I value her life above obeying my Heavenly Father?*

Adam knew exactly what he was doing. Thinking within himself that God would somehow make everything right again, he succumbed to the treacherous temptation to disobey.

He took the fruit from her hand, bit into it, chewed, and swallowed.

Immediately, both he and Eve became aware of evil. Previously protected, now they were fully exposed to the lure of sin.

Looking at each other they instantly became conscious of the fact that they were naked. *Who else can see us?* There had to be unseen witnesses in the sprit world all around. [47] Surely all could see their nudity.

Embarrassment with their exposed situation overshadowed the shame they felt. Gathering fig leaves, Eve put her creative skills to work and helped Adam stitch together some body coverings. Using a quill from

---

[47]   We are surrounded with a cloud of witnesses. Hebrews 12:1

the porcupine as a needle and plant fibers as thread she fashioned some suitable clothing. *Yes, this will work.*

They felt better after donning the clothes; yet before the day was over the garments began to dry and shrivel. Fear crept into their psyches and completely took over, dominating their thoughts.

Will THE FATHER find out? We can't let him know what we did. Where can we hide?[48]

In the throne room the angels watched sadly as Adam and Eve failed the test. *Adam is no match for the wily Lucifer.* He'd succumbed to the temptation to sin in an attempt to protect his wife. Oh, the deceitfulness of Satan in misusing God-given instincts for his reprobate purposes!

In Adam's fall the hope for mankind to make consistently right decisions ceased. They didn't have the strength or wisdom necessary to defeat the evil one. But there's always hope in the Creator of Love. A plan had already been formulated to offer forgiveness as well as restoration for all.

A quick meeting was called and all pertinent information was revealed to the sons about Adam's sin. "Now it's not possible for them to live forever in human form. The mandate is clear. As warned, before this day[49] is over both Adam and Eve must die."

It took only one sin for the door of death to open. Adam's DNA was now tainted and would affect everyone born after him. Super-human, uncontaminated blood was needed to absolve the world of sin.

---

[48] Story of Adam and Eve taken from Genesis, chapters 1-2.

[49] One day in Heaven is 1,000 years. As promised, neither reached their 1,000-year birthday on Earth.

"The tendency of mankind to sin will increase from this point onward."

"How can this trend be reversed?"

"Through his love HE'll win them back."

"But legally, the price for their disobedience must be paid."

"How?"

The Father relayed to them the restoration plan. "Mankind needs a Savior, one who'll be willing to live as a human among them, be tempted in all points like them, yet live his life totally without sin.[50] His perfect life will prevent him from being under the law of sin and death. Therefore, by dying a sinner's death, his innocence will pay for the freedom of all those under bondage to evil and its god."

This was the Father's plan? To take the blame and pay the price? The room was quiet. *Who would be able to make this happen?*

Lucifer was powerful; the Father had given him authority with massive amounts of control. This could not be automatically reversed. Liberation had to be done legally, without an open loophole, and with nothing to cause questioning about the tactics involved. Only ONE with divine intelligence and tremendous strength would be able to accomplish this.

As the discussion continued amongst the sons, THE WORD mulled over the possibilities in his mind. He knew it was not a light thing to volunteer for the task. There'd be temptations—devious, strong temptations. There'd also be pain and abandonment, aspects not allowed in Heaven. The volunteer would experience temptation in the same

---

[50]   Hebrews 4:15

way as the rest of mankind, yet he must remain undeceived and without sin.

He'd never experienced sin or any of Lucifer's evil inventions. Everything about it was the antithesis of the good he knew and went against every fiber of goodness in his being. This undertaking would require some thought. *There is already a blood ransom owed for Adam's liberation. Who will pay it for him?*

Jeric, Jano and the others watching in the archive room were silent as they witnessed the dilemma. The tragedy of wrong choice was no less dramatic in the present than it was in Adam's day.

Watching from the archives the subsequent gathering of the two-thirds of Heaven's inhabitants, they witnessed the eagerness of Michael's and Gabriel's angels to help with the restoration process. Lining up, they were given jobs: some were assigned to work as warriors, some as messengers, and others as personal guardian angels.

But still a special volunteer was needed. "Who will go to Earth as a human baby, grow up in a sinful world, resist all temptations of Lucifer and die to give his life as a ransom for the rest?"

"Anyone?"

There was silence as they all pondered the question. *Would I be able to live undeceived in a world where deception dominates? Can I defeat the power of evil by one-hundred percent adherence to the law? What about the deceivability factor? As a limited human will I be able to detect Lucifer's cunning tricks? Adam and Eve failed . . .*

Their peers had already shown they were no match for the cunning Lucifer. The only one qualified for such a task would be the all-knowing Father Himself.

"Who will defeat the powerful god of evil on his own turf?" All of Heaven remained silent as the question hung in space. [51]

As the great assembly watched, One came forward. He was magnificent, with eyes like fire; a form of God Himself.

THE WORD.

Made in the image of his Father, his countenance was brighter than the stars. It was HE who graciously volunteered, willing to pay the painful price. It would be the highest act of love ever performed.

The decision was made. He'd been there from the beginning with the Father when the foundations of the earth were put together.[52] He knew the plan and understood the strength it would take. The embodiment of the WORD OF GOD, he was not only willing, but was not deceivable. He would become the Savior of mankind

The purpose was set; the motion of activity went forward. Redemption was the goal as the coordinated preparations were made. Before the evening get-together with Adam, the Father had put his plan into motion.

---

[51] Silence for one-half hour in Heaven would be equivalent to twenty years, six months and twelve days of Earth time.

[52] Eph 3:9

Chapter 8

Increase of Disobedience

Be sure your sin will find you out.

Numbers 32:23

Adam had been given the first opportunity but he, along with Eve, failed. Though the world had been cleansed and carefully prepared before the great test, sin entered it through Adam's disobedience. Now sin, like mold, would grow and double in strength with each passing generation. Its grip would have to be broken.

Adam and Eve's eyes were opened, but not in the way they'd expected. Deceived into believing they could achieve a shortcut back to Heaven as godlike beings, they'd failed miserably in fulfilling their goal. Afraid, they hid among the trees.

But God had already put his plan into motion. Innocent blood was shed as HE made clothing out of animal skins—the first leather britches.

Soon the couple felt a cool breeze rustling through the trees, a sign that indicated the Father's presence.

"Adam, where are you?"

"I heard your voice and was afraid. We hid because we're naked."

"Did you eat the forbidden fruit?"

"The woman you gave handed me the fruit, so I ate it."

"The snake deceived me."

No longer talking, the snake just watched, its tongue moving slowly in and out of its mouth. His silvery voice was forever gone.

"Adam, no longer will your garden grow easily by itself; you'll have to battle deep-rooted brambles, weeds and thorns throughout the heat of the day."

"Eve, when you give birth it will always be with excruciating pain. Even then, your desire will be for your husband."

"Serpent, your beauty will be repulsive to every female on Earth. No longer will you walk the earth but will slither on the ground."

Lucifer, gloating on his gain, realized he'd not only caused Adam to sin, but also devastation to the poor animal that had the misfortune of being chosen for his scheme. Evil was the most fulfilling to him when it caused destruction to any of God's creation. "Yes! I've changed the world forever," he thought smugly.

The I AM continued talking to Adam and Eve. "As a result of your sin, you may no longer live in this beautiful garden."

Why?

"It's dangerous. If you eat of the Tree of Life now, you'll forever remain in your present sinful condition."

As Adam and Eve pondered these words, the FATHER presented them with the gift of beautifully crafted leather clothing.

"Here, you can put these on."

Adam examined the garments, the source of the material uppermost in his mind. The VOICE, so full of love and compassion again softly spoke. "They died so that you could be covered."

Yielding to sin caused much more devastation than the pair of them initially thought. The heavenly laws could not be broken; therefore the restoration of fellowship with the Father had to be paid for through the shedding of innocent blood.

Adam and Eve left the garden together, knowing their lives had forever changed. There was forgiveness available, yet how was it to be accessed? Through an animal sacrifice? They were, by necessity, eager to learn what they must do to receive a pardon for their sin.

Regardless of their new determination toward right choices, their initial disobedience came with dire consequences. Life became difficult, with weeds growing faster than the produce in the garden. Cattle now often died of disease, weather elements constantly worked against Adam's sweat equity, and arguments between them occurred far too often. It was hard to be pleasant when exhausted, sick, irritated, or in pain. Mosquitoes now caused itching, bees stung, and poisonous weeds made life miserable.

As life got harder, Eve became consumed with regrets. Adam often tried to console her, but usually gave up when he saw that nothing worked. Eventually he simply left her alone during her bouts of crying.

It was during this time that Adam noticed Eve's midsection growing. This was a much-needed diversion from their now difficult and demanding life schedule. Not missing the significance of her expanding girth, he mentally noted the progress of this first human pregnancy on Earth.

Notwithstanding, Adam also fell into a deep depression as the full weight of reality hit him. His disobedience had opened the door for sin to affect his children as well as all future generations. The very moment he took the first forbidden bite he knew he'd failed.

"It would have happened anyway," Eve tried to console him.

"You were my responsibility. I needed to protect you. I should have stayed strong. I didn't comprehend at the time that I could have died in your place."

"Adam, don't be so hard on yourself. Our Heavenly Father knows our limitations. I am deceivable . . . no two ways around it."

Adam gently put his arm around her. "I love you so much! I would have gladly given my life for you, yet I went about it wrong. The enemy is strong, and much cleverer than either one of us."

"God knows and understands. He'll make a way for us to be redeemed."

When overwhelmed with guilt, Adam usually handled this by working himself into exhaustion. He became obsessed with thoughts of everything being restored back to normal again. *Will it ever happen? Is it even possible? Is there anything we can do to make it right?*

It was a long time before either Adam or Eve could sleep through the night without waking up in a cold sweat.

Chapter 9

The Deception of Jealousy

Don't be deceived; God is not mocked: for whatever a man sows, that shall he also reap.

Gal. 6:7

Soon baby Cain was born, joined not too long afterward by brother Abel. Though parenting them was a new experience, it was also a natural one. Instincts of protection for Adam were strong; maternal instincts were even stronger for Eve. The family bond was solid, causing contentment even though their home was now outside of Eden.[53]

As the boys grew they tussled and played together, accepting their world as they'd found it. Cain was a gentle boy who loved to grow things in the field. He would often help Adam with the hoeing and weeding and was always excited to discover a new edible plant. He especially enjoyed experimenting with different methods to see how big he could grow his vegetables.

Abel took over the caring of the animals. He soon discovered which species were easiest to raise, which ones were the tastiest for meat, and which ones could be grown

---

[53] Eden was the name of the original garden from which they'd been banned. Genesis 2:15

for clothing purposes. It wasn't long before he had a healthy flock of sheep and a strong herd of cows.

Cows gave milk, which could be made into butter and cheese. Sheep gave wool for clothing and meat for eating. As he worked daily with them, he particularly enjoyed playing with the cute little lambs.

Having learned about the need for a blood sacrifice from their parents, the boys prepared to fulfill their sacrificial requirements. Abel chose the most perfect lamb from the flock for his altar. It was tough, killing the baby before laying it upon the stones, but he did so in obedience to the plan.

Cain thought within himself: *I won't take one of Abel's lambs because that represents his labor, not mine. I'll give my largest and best produce as an offering.*

The day came when both boys built altars. Excitedly, Cain placed his fruit and vegetables on the stones while Abel arranged his bloodied little lamb. Cain thought smugly: *My way is better; no animal has to die.*

As smoke poured out from the altars, Abel's smoke ascended straight to Heaven. Cain's smoke, however, just smoldered on the stones before falling to the ground.

Hmm. Maybe I didn't lay the fruit right. Why isn't it burning properly? He adjusted the mess. Soon a burned odor permeated the area, with the smoke still rolling down off the altar. Abel's smoke, on the other hand, continued to shoot skyward from the meat.

Disappointing.

Abel looked his way. "Go get a lamb from my flock. You need blood for the sacrifice."

What does he know? The showoff! "My sacrifice is just as good as yours, even better because no animal has to suffer."

God isn't fair! He honors Abel but not me. Why? I work harder, I give more to the family, and am definitely smarter than he is. Yet now he's accepted while I'm rejected

Cain wouldn't look at his brother. He was more than embarrassed; he was outraged that God would not honor all his hard work!

Unknown to him, a standard for salvation had to be firmly established. Only through the shedding of innocent blood could the sins of mankind be atoned for. The lamb's death was a type and shadow of the ONE who was to come. Those who sacrificed a lamb were, in faith, putting their sins on the tab of the future SACRIFICIAL LAMB of God.

The I AM didn't want Cain to miss out on salvation through his ignorance of not doing what was needed. Yet Cain, instead of correcting his actions to meet the requirements of redemption, chose to be jealous of his brother. He didn't see the big picture of eventual salvation for all of mankind. He only saw his temporal disappointment and opted to feel rejected as a person.

As Abel's love and commitment to God's ways grew strong, Cain's jealousy escalated into hatred. Eventually Cain's anger was so immense that he couldn't even be polite, let alone say a civil word to his brother. Exasperated with the situation, Abel finally approached him.

"What's your problem? I'm ready to talk about it."

"You are, are you?"

"Sure, if it helps."

"Meet me in the field. Then I'll let you know what's on my mind." *I hate him!*

Abel was eager to restore fellowship with his brother; he missed the fun they used to have together. All he ever saw now was Cain's dark, malicious face. Anxious to get things settled he waited for Cain in the field.

"What's the matter, Cain?"

"You think you're better than me, don't you."

"No I don't!"

"Liar!" Without another word Cain brought out the tool he used to hoe his garden. Beating it over Abel's head, his anger reached a passion that surprised even him.

"Stop, Cain. You're hurting me!"

Cain couldn't stop, for something evil had unleashed within him an overwhelming rage. It was a devil-inspired moment, one where he lost complete control; for he allowed the evil from the dark side to thoroughly control his thoughts and actions. In complete overkill, he didn't stop beating Abel until his body was nothing but a bloody mass.

Breathless from exertion, his anger finally appeased, he now looked at what he'd done. Abel, like the lamb on the altar, was dead.

Suddenly frightened, Cain looked around. *Did anyone see me?* No one was in sight. Using his hoe to dig into the dirt, he buried Abel's body in a shallow grave. Covering him up, the ground looked just as before. He determined to keep his actions secret.

Now that Abel was gone, Cain had no one to blame for the desolation he felt. *Does God know what I've done? It's his fault, after all, for He was the one who rejected me. I did my best, yet God overlooked me and honored my stupid little brother.*

Walking away from the field, he felt some of the vengeful anger leave. What had he done? *Nothing that wasn't deserved.* He would tell no one.

That night he heard a voice "Cain, Cain."

"What?"

"Where is your brother?"

"How should I know? Am I supposed to take care of him?"

"Abel's blood cries to me from the ground." Startled, Cain knew he'd been found out.

"Your act of murder has opened up an ugly potential for even worse sin than before."

"If anyone finds out, they'll kill me."

"I'll put a mark on you; no one will touch you, but you may not live with your family anymore."

Cain was marked and banished from his childhood home.

All Cain's descendants would now be born with an ever-increasing propensity for hatred and rage, thanks to his murder-tainted DNA.

Chapter 10

The Generations of Man

All the days that Adam lived were nine hundred and thirty years: and he died.

Genesis 5:5

The first human death had occurred. Righteous Abel was welcomed into paradise, having won the battle over evil by obedience and faith in the required sacrificial lamb. His entrance to Heaven was put on the tab of IOU's as a ransom to be paid. Someone would need to make good the debt.

Meanwhile, Cain's behavior changed so much that Eve was beside herself with worry. He'd become deceitful, angry and disrespectful. Helpless, she could only watch in disbelief as he rebelled against everything she and Adam had taught him.

Heartbroken over his conduct, she at the same time felt responsible for it. Their perfect world had changed for the worse and Eve didn't know how to reverse the downward spiral.

That Cain withheld knowledge regarding Abel's whereabouts was apparent, yet he refused to discuss the matter. Abel's absence became a daily topic of heated discussion until the day Cain announced he was moving with his wife to a place at the east of Eden named Nod; it was a bittersweet relief to see him go.[54]

Observing the subsequent intensity of corruption and murder that gained a stronghold with Cain's descendants, Eve was overwhelmed at her lack of power to eradicate it from their lives. After many more years, however, she found peace with the conclusion that she had no choice but to hope in the mercy of a loving God.

I will trust in Him and in HIS plan for redemption.

Saddened with the now-known knowledge of Abel's murder and the subsequent banishment of Cain, Adam and Eve were nevertheless comforted when another son was born.

"He resembles you, Adam."

"Well, what do you know!"

They named him Seth, which means "appointed one." A younger image of his father, Seth was a great joy to his parents. Obedient and conscientious, he was one with which THE FATHER took great delight.

The generations of man will descend from this son.[55]

The first "day" of 1,000 years was almost over and Adam's season as mankind had ended. At age 930 Adam took his last breath and died.

As Adam's spirit entered into the transport tunnel, he knew distinctly he'd failed the test. God had given him a chance to have a part in mankind's redemption, yet he'd not been able to withstand the temptations of the enemy. But he was not without hope. Not only had he, by faith, taken part in the required sacrifices of atonement, he'd also observed

---

[54]   The Bible does not say from where he got his wife. It is assumed that his wife was a sister. See Gen 4:17.

[55]   All Cain's descendants died in the flood.

his godly son Seth teaching his children and grandchildren the ways of righteousness.

Maybe one of his descendants will be able to pay the price for our redemption.

Chapter 11
The Redemption Plan

I will help you, says the Lord your Redeemer, the Holy One of Israel.

Isa 41:14

When sin entered the world, sickness and death also entered. As one by one the banished were born into the world of mankind, each generation found it harder and harder to live a healthy, sinless life. None were completely successful, though a few came close. Only two righteous men went straight to Heaven without having to go through the dying process.[56]

Meanwhile the sons of God met together to watch the progress of the test transpiring on Earth. Observing the families as mankind began to multiply upon the face[57] of the earth, they saw that their daughters were attractive; some chose human wives for themselves.[58] This resulted in giants being born within the human population.[59]

---

[56] Enoch and Elijah. See Gen 5:24; Heb 11:5; 2 Kings 2:11
[57] Note the usage of "face" vs. "pit."
[58] Gen. 6:2
[59] Is it possible that some of the "sons" lived on Earth incognito? See Hebrews 13:2

These giants became men of renown, strong, doing exploits. But this was not the plan of the Father, for mankind needed to solve the tests of life without giants to distract them. They needed one giant, a heavenly GIANT, who wouldn't succumb to the temptations of evil, but would be a willing and perfect sacrifice as the Lamb of God. The sin and sickness of the world had to be taken away through one method only. God's redemptive plan had to be carried out in full and would not work with any shortcut.

One day the Sons of God met together with the Lord, and Lucifer came with them. He'd tried everything he could think of to cause a righteous man named Job to sin, but had failed miserably. The reason? Job adamantly trusted in God's plan for redemption. Job not only refused to give in to Lucifer's manipulations but prayed for the ones who'd troubled him.[60]

During the worst of his misery, God asked Job: "Where were you when the earth was formed?" There was only one answer, and righteous Job knew what it was: he'd been sitting in darkness in the shadow of death, deep in the depths of the Pit.[61] His reply was the battle cry for everyone who trusted in the redemption that was to come: By faith he shouted:

"I KNOW THAT MY REDEEMER LIVES!"[62] All Heaven rejoiced at his answer, for it confirmed that at least one human understood the plan.

On the second heavenly day the I AM spoke to THE WORD: "I've put together ten basic precepts of behavior

---

[60] For more on this story, read <u>Dark Stars of The Twilight</u> © 2009 by Marilyn Olson
[61] Job 33:29-30
[62] Job 19:25

that will instruct mankind to live righteously with their limited knowledge on Earth."

"The first—"

"—is the most important, to worship only the I AM. In addition, they must not use my name in a non-reverent way. They must not make images of gods for the purposes of worship. They must keep the Sabbath day holy. They must not kill, must not commit adultery, and must not steal or lie. They must honor their parents, and not covet what others have."

"You're right. These ten should do it. Keeping these commandments will convey the basic concept of "good.""

In the days to follow these Ten Commandments became the guide of mankind to separate right from wrong. The godly judges of Earth wisely utilized these ten mandates in order to make correct decisions. Though justice ruled for a time in the lives of the chosen,[63] there was still something missing: the spirit of loving the truth.

"Search throughout the earth, find me a man who understands my heart.[64]

The Word walked the earth, and found what he was looking for. He was a boy watching his father's sheep, singing "The Lord is My Shepherd . . ."

"This young man has it right. My ancestral line will continue through him; the Kingdom will be firmly established with his descendants."[65]

THE WORD watched in interest as David the shepherd become the most beloved king of Israel. Not only

---

[63] "Chosen" refers to the lineage of Christ, which came through Abraham, Isaac, and Jacob. See Acts 3: 24-25
[64] 1 Sam 13:14
[65] 1 Chronicles 17:11-14

was his worship rich with music, singing and dancing to the Lord, but his decisions toward others were fair as well as merciful.

His example of true worship will strengthen my people.

Yet as the humans of Earth continually fought against righteousness on every front, evil reigned in many of the tribes of Earth. Deceived and manipulated, humans—even with the written Ten Commandments—were no match for the craftiness of Lucifer and his cohorts. Though the standard of the Ten Commandments had been set, there had to be a better way to implement it.

It wasn't an easy fix. The failure of mankind to perfectly keep the commandments became for them a prison, evoking shame and despair. No one was powerful enough to keep them perfectly, as Adam himself so miserably proved. Therefore the Savior as the unblemished lamb could not be of the seed of Adam, for sin had polluted his DNA. A new, sinless strain had to be introduced to the world.

As the generations came and went, the godliest with the least amount of sin in their bloodline were chosen to father the descendants to continue the line.[66] Abraham, Isaac, Jacob, David—these were men who could be trusted to continue the requirements needed for God's plan.

With this lineage in place the ancestral line for the birth of the Savior was established.

The fourth day was about over. It was time to separate the light from the darkness.

The Day of Redemption had come.

---

[66]   See Galatians 3:18-19 The inheritance was given to Abraham"—till the seed should come to whom the promise was made."

Chapter 12

The Son on Earth

He sent redemption to his people.

Psalms 111:9

In the I AM and his Word was life. This life was LIGHT to mankind. Jesus, the SON of God, was the Volunteer who chose to undertake the sacrifice of redemption. He would pay the price for all humanity, Jew and Gentile alike.[67]

When the earth was black with darkness on the face of the deep, this LIGHT shined in: the darkness didn't understand it. This Light is the true light, which lights every man that comes into the world. He came into the world that was made by him, but the world didn't recognize him.[68]

Why?

The story of Jesus, from a first hand account, was about to begin. Breathless in anticipation, Korel and his group of friends could only watch in wonder as they experienced the life of Jesus, the Savior of the world.

Mankind had been on Earth for 4,000 years, well over half the time allotted for the great test. The Word, willing as

---

[67] The Jews are the descendants of Abraham, Isaac, and Jacob. Everyone else is a "Gentile." See Romans 2:9-10

[68] Text from John 1:1-13

well as worthy for the mission, was notified to return to the Highest Heaven. He bid goodbye to his companions and quickly made the journey.[69]

As his personage appeared on the screen of the archives the room erupted: "There he is!" All in the room were entranced, for the moment had finally come to view HIS personal earth story.

Jano looked at Korel. "Virtual?" he asked.

"Yes." It was settled.[70] They would witness the life of Jesus as seen through his eyes.

What an amazing adventure lay ahead! They settled back, took a breath, and pressed the green button. Soon they found themselves witnessing the greatest story ever told.

The Word

Called into the Father's inner chamber, The Word noticed the others standing respectfully along the hallway. *Are they aware of what's about to transpire?*

The fact that he'd been summoned with a distinct urgency did not concern him. He had enjoyed creating the sun, moon and stars with the Father. He'd walked the earth, observing the unfolding of God's plan there.[71] Still, he knew he had yet to fulfill a very important piece to the puzzle that had been reserved until this moment.

---

[69] Jesus came down from Heaven rather than up from the Pit. In John 8:23 Jesus said "You are from below, I am from above."

[70] In the archives it's possible to experience the life as if you are that person. For more details, read The Twinkling, © 2008.

[71] Dan 3:25 mentions the Son of God. See also Dan 10:16.

Entering in the place of pure Love was always a delight. He thoroughly enjoyed being in the presence of his Father.

"How are you, Apple of My Eye?" HIS loving voice resounded through the marble halls.

Smiling, The Word approached the throne. "Delighted, as always. It's time, isn't it—"

"—to enter the world as mankind. You'll be born as a baby with no prior knowledge of pre-earth events. I've chosen loving parents for you. Growing up under their watchful care your physical maturity will be just like any other young Israeli boy. But there'll be a difference. Your DNA will contain no ancestral sins."

"Though your mother will be human, having descended from Adam's line, the DNA strain needed from the father's side will come directly from me. As a result, your blood will be as pure and sinless as Adam's was originally. You'll be both Son of Man and Son of God."[72]

"—A legality required to fulfill the redemption of mankind."

"Your earthly parents are also descendants of King David—"

"—fulfilling certain promises to Israel and his descendants."

"Yes." The Father was quiet for a moment, before continuing. "Though many in this chosen race of people have followed my commandments, the seeds of evil have sprouted and spread throughout all the earth. There is none righteous anywhere; all have sinned and are in need of a Savior.[73]

---

[72] Mark 1:1, Luke 1:35, Luke 19:10
[73] Romans 3:23; 5:12

"From what I've observed, I have no doubt the rest of the generations of man will follow the same path to destruction."

"They have the Ten Commandments—"

"—but so many rules have been added to them that the original intent is almost unrecognizable."

"What do you suggest?"

"Simplify them. Narrow them down to 'Love the Father with all your heart, and love each other as yourself.'"

"That's good. Simplicity is what's needed here. Use the same approach in telling stories to teach truths of the kingdom. As they believe and grasp onto the Word of Truth, enemy strongholds will be broken."

"There are so many people to reach in one lifetime . . ."

"Start with twelve men; teach them in-depth about the Kingdom. The Word will spread out from there. Those who are truly my people will want to do right. If not, they'll continue to do the deeds of their lying 'father' who is a murderer from the beginning."[74]

Pausing a poignant moment before continuing, the Father spoke softly: "As a human you'll experience pain, sorrow, rejection—"

"—I can endure anything you allow to happen to me."

"There are other things that sin brought: disease, crime, death—"

"—I'm ready to deal with them!" The Word was adamant in his purpose. "I'm more than ready. I'm anxious to bring healing as well as to restore life!"

The FATHER could see his SON'S determination to not be limited by pending humanness. HIS resolve to break the power gripping the fallen was strong.

---

[74] John 8:44

The appointed time came; the sons whispered "good-bye" to the Lamb of God. Soon a baby named "Jesus" was born on Earth to a virgin named Mary.[75]

---

[75] For complete story, see the book of Matthew from the Holy Bible.

Chapter 13
Jesus' Childhood

Signs and wonders may be done by the name of your holy child Jesus.

Acts 4: 30

Life was busy and happy at the home of Joseph and Mary. Jesus woke up each day with the smell of fresh bread permeating the house. His mom had to be the best cook in the village! Every morning as the sun would peak over the horizon Mary could be seen walking to the village to buy grain and fresh food for the day. What she didn't buy, she grew in her well-kept garden. She made bread every morning during the week, and enough on Friday to last for the Sabbath.

His hard-working dad was also a strong presence in the home. Gentle and kind, his responsibilities toward his family predicated every decision he made. His love for Mary was obvious in his tender smile toward her and loving words to others about her.

Oldest of the children, Jesus felt secure in his home. The many younger siblings that came along in time were a tribute to the health of his parents. Fighting? Certainly, but he was a good referee; his siblings could depend upon him to settle an argument between them fairly. He always perceived exactly what happened, totally understood the situation, and knew how to repair the tension between them.

There was some expected jealousy, especially from his younger brother James. Next in age to Jesus, James couldn't compete with either his intelligence or his sense of fairness in dealing with others. Sibling rivalry—a normal state of affairs for most families—was also in theirs.

Jesus loved his brothers and sisters just as he loved his parents. As the oldest he naturally took on the role of the dominant firstborn, having an instinct to protect them from harm.

Even as a child Jesus knew he was different from others. He preferred to do what was right and did so at all times; never did he entertain even a thought of violating the healthy conscience with which he'd been born. This got him into occasional trouble with his friends and siblings.

Think about it . . . to always be right, to never be wrong, to never give in to the temptations and youthful mischievousness that plagues the rest of youth . . . this was his manner.

There were times when the thought of a prank gave him enjoyment; however, he never participated in one if it was tinged even slightly with drawing anxiety from the victim. Yet he had a great sense of humor, often delighting his friends and family with his playfulness towards them.

As a child he didn't fully understand all that was ahead of him; but even during those years he experienced a sense of oneness with his Heavenly Father. Jesus subconsciously knew who he was and this knowledge grew with him as he matured.[76]

---

[76]   John 8:23

He didn't question his calling, but only sought to continually learn more about it. Even if initially not fully understanding everything, obedience to his Heavenly Father's guidance was the way he overcame the evil influence of the world's way of thinking. He continually sought to more fully concentrate on hearing and obeying this gentle voice. Daily as he communicated with HIM, HE became his closest companion.

One day Mary took him aside. "Jesus, I want to show you something." From under the bed she brought out an ornate, sweet-smelling box and a decorative cloth pouch. Reaching into the bag, she pulled out three golden coins—all that remained. "When you were a baby, kings came from other countries to worship you. They'd followed a star placed in the heavens, knowing it would take them to where you were. These are some of the gifts they brought." She related to him the details of his unique birth.

As he examined the empty box left by the visitors, he marveled at the loving heavenly provision. Not only had THE FATHER confirmed who he was through a star in the sky, but his parents had been able to buy their house and shop because of the gifts.

The next day as he helped his father in the shop, Joseph remarked: "Son, soon you'll reach your twelfth birthday. One year from that day you will be recognized as a man. As you know, there are certain responsibilities as well as privileges that come with that recognition."

Jesus smiled, for he already knew what his father was about to say.

Joseph continued, "At this time you'll be allowed to accompany us to the temple in Jerusalem." His parents had gone there every year since he could remember; at last he'd be able to join them. He eagerly counted the days until the journey.

As the day of departure approached, his excitement grew. He recognized he would be in the temple built to his FATHER'S specifications; a heavenly structural design that housed the Holy of Holies within its gates.

Soon the day arrived and he, along with his parents, joined others from the village to travel together. Jesus and his young companions laughed and played as they walked, enjoying the freedom of the adventure. As evening fell the first day they unloaded the tents from the donkey and quickly set them up. *Sleeping under the stars together is a treat. Let the adults use the tents!*

Camping each night and walking during the day was a slow process, but one of intense pleasure. Before long they climbed the last hill that led to Jerusalem.

Jesus

The temple before me was majestic! Entering through the gates, something welled up within me. This was my Father's House . . . .

Looking around, I saw the activity—some of it godly and pleasing to God, and some of it worldly with thieves and con artists using the temple as a means of defrauding its worshippers. *I didn't expect this.*

We entered the courtyard and continued on through the entrance. In the room to my right the Pharisees and doctors of the law were deep in study. Noticing the scrolls with the Word of God open on the table I knew: *This is where I want to be!*

Taking my place on the floor, I quietly listened as the discussion grew animated and even heated at times. At one point I raised my hand, making a comment about the scripture passage in question.

Suddenly the room was silent, for I'd asked a question not only pertinent to the discussion, but its answer provided keen insight to the group. Eyebrows raised, the bearded teachers turned around to see who had voiced the query. Noticing me, they were more than a little perplexed.

Who is this young man?

They were aware of the strong prophetic word Simeon had spoken over a baby twelve years ago. Every day until his death, he insisted he'd held the Messiah in his arms. The mystery child had not been seen since.[77]

Is this him? He's the right age.

Gathering around me while focusing on my person, the questions began in earnest.

---

[77] Luke 2:25

So excited was I to be conversing with these great men of the law that I didn't notice the passage of time; we talked late into the night and into the next day.

Meanwhile my parents had moved from this room to another, assuming I was with their party. Even while traveling home the following day they didn't notice I was missing; I'd always been, in their eyes, where I was supposed to be.

Eventually realizing I wasn't in the group, Mom began to cry. *What's happened? It can't be time already!* Though she knew I was special, she'd also been told that "a sword would pierce" her soul. *Not yet!* At my present tender age she still wanted to protect me from the world.

Though deeply concerned, Dad attempted to reassure Mom that all would be well as the two of them left the group and hurried back to Jerusalem.

Where is Jesus?

Anxiously they returned to the temple, retracing their every step. Finding a large crowd of teachers in the main hall, they quickly walked past them. But then they heard my young, strong voice amongst the gathering.

"Jesus?" Mom turned around, her worried face lined with grief and perplexity.

"This young boy is extremely intelligent, understanding way above his age level. His interest in and understanding of spiritual things has amazed us," spoke a highly regarded teacher.

Dad, however, was in no mood to be complimentary. Giving me a sharp look, he asked, "Didn't you know your mother would be worried? Why have you done this?" Mom with tears streaming down her face grabbed me, hugging me with all her strength.

"Why did you look for me? Don't you know I must focus on my Father's business?"[78] I truly was perplexed. Mom had told me numerous times who my biological Father was. Dad had also relayed to me that I was soon to be considered a man. *Didn't they think I'd been listening?*

Sorry for inadvertently causing them emotional pain, I hugged them both while inwardly deciding to communicate better in the future. The last thing I wanted to do was to cause grief to my dear parents.

---

[78] Luke 2:49

Chapter 14
Growing Tall, Gaining Wisdom

And Jesus increased in wisdom and stature, and in favor with God and man.

Luke 2:52

Frustrated, and a bit fearful in letting him out of their sight—for he'd been the target of death by a powerful king in the past—his parents forgot who he was for a moment, ready to reproach. His surprising words, however, brought them quickly back to reality. Yes, he was preparing for a mission, but the time for it was premature.

He needs to be home and protected until he fully reaches adulthood.

Teenage years brought about a different type of newness. Maturing in body as well as mind, Jesus experienced all the growth surprises that his brothers did. Yet, nothing fazed him; he continued to be kind, patient, and honorable to his parents. With an inborn sense of purpose that felt right, he determined to never break the bond of goodness that had hold of him.

Joseph, a skilled carpenter, had an excellent reputation that extended far beyond their village. Jesus loved to work in the shop with him, creating beautiful pieces of furniture. Beds, chairs, tables, desks, and many other items were perfectly crafted with his young hands. Mary often watched him as he worked, marveling at the gift in the Son she was given.

The family never lacked for new work orders as Jesus and his dad completed each project with precision and good craftsmanship. All of their customers were astonished at Jesus' skill and the perfection in his work. People came from all over Galilee to buy furniture from Joseph's little shop.

Jesus' younger brothers would often accompany him in search of suitable wood for the carpentry work. Taking the donkey and cart to the nearby forests was an arduous, all-day event. On occasion they'd find a fallen tree in the village and would offer their services to remove it, saving themselves a day's labor. Regardless of how they acquired the wood, cutting and transporting it was an enjoyable activity for all of them.

James and Joses didn't mind the hard work—it had a good side effect of increasing their strength as well as their physical muscle mass. This was noticed not only by their friends but also the potential employers in the village.

Those in the archive room watched as the boy Jesus grew strong and handsome over the years, increasing in wisdom as well as in height.[79] Everyone in his life was impressed with him; he was trustworthy, fair in his dealings, and by far the favorite babysitter of his younger siblings. Physically strong, he'd become somewhat of a legend when it came to races and other games played in the streets.

These years were filled with numerous weddings, funerals, births, and mitzvahs. Along with these events, the work in the shop kept them all busy.

---

[79]   Luke 2:52

Jesus dearly loved the Father with all his heart. As the knowledge of his purpose grew within him, however, his heart was often grieved with the sin of the world. Faith was so natural for him that he became increasingly perplexed at the lack of faith found in God's people. He struggled to understand the limitations of others—he himself had no doubt he could remove mountains if he so desired. But with his parent's gentle teaching and example, he learned to function within the limited world of mankind.

Jesus

It astounded me, but I said very little about it. Growing up with brothers James and Joses, I understood too well how feelings could get hurt so I usually kept my mouth shut. Still, at times I was totally amazed at the lack of conviction exhibited by my peers.

Sure, I was tempted in every area, same as anyone else my age. Yet, unlike the other boys, I didn't give in to the temptations. It simply wasn't in my nature to sin.

It was in my brother's nature, however, and as a result of not being able to compete with me, I was made the butt of some jokes and snide remarks. Regardless, nothing could stop me from loving my siblings and eventually my attitude toward them superseded any jealous thoughts they had toward me.

We had fun as we grew up together. Laughing, playing and enjoying each other's company, my childhood years were full of enjoyable activity and good memories.

My parents often talked late into the night, discussing different options available to them. Sometimes I could overhear their muffled conversations: "He's noticed in the neighborhood: 'The carpenter's son, so handsome, so kind, so good at his trade!'" Many times they were approached with possible marriage contracts from well-meaning parents of available daughters.

Joseph had been chosen by God for the responsibility of guiding as well as protecting me in my formative years. He'd been an excellent father to me. Hesitantly, one day, he brought up a sensitive subject: "Son, you've reached the age where most parents would arrange a marriage." Here he stopped, looking at me quizzically.

I knew what he was thinking. A marriage would be nice . . . to want to hold a beautiful girl in a gentle embrace was an instinctive desire planted within every healthy human male. I was no different in that regard, desiring to love and cherish a special someone. But I quickly put those thoughts out of my mind, for I realized marriage was not for me. A wife would be distracting as well as present difficult situations of temptation, as Adam and other "sons of God" had previously demonstrated.[80] Besides, I had work to do and marriage would hinder me from that effort.

"Father, you know the answer.—"

"—Hear me out. Your mother has been a delight to me; how could I have functioned without her? It's not good for man to live alone.[81] He needs a helpmate. And you, Son . . ." he choked up, not able to continue.

My father was a good man, a hard worker, gentle in spirit, and righteous in his dealings. He loved me, and the fact that I'd became more skilled than he at carpentry only made him prouder of me. He had my best interests at heart; yet, we both knew the answer:

"I cannot now, nor can I ever marry."

[80] Gen. 5:4
[81] Gen. 2:18

Joseph looked at me for a long time, nodded his head, and patted me on the shoulder.

"I understand." I held him for a moment, our earthly roles reversed. My earthly father was a saint. My heavenly Father had chosen for me the best of mankind to oversee my upbringing.

As I watched some of my siblings marry and start families, I grew impatient to begin the ministry for which God had prepared me. I continued, however, to submit to my parent's authority as I waited until the time was right. Though there were some occasional pangs of loneliness, I stayed resolute to my calling.

Mom was a gracious hostess, many times inviting neighbors and friends over for dinner. One of these friends had a daughter who was engaged to be married. Our family was invited to the wedding. The engaged couple had grown up in our village. I knew them very well; we'd played together as children. The girl was also a friend of my younger sister Salome.

"Judith's wedding is coming this spring," Mother reminded me. "Make sure the boys are ready." I knew what she meant: "Make sure your brothers know the dances."

I not only loved to dance but was also quick to learn every dance step. With each movement having a meaning, putting the steps together was a great way to dance in praise and worship to God. Some of the dances could be traced clear back to our forefather King David. I was the one who usually taught these dances to my brothers.

My family enjoyed these celebrations; the food and dancing, connecting with good friends and joyful music not only gave us time together as a family but also provided a change of pace from our work in the shop.

These were memorable years.

Chapter 15
Jesus Baptism and Temptation

*I have baptized you with water: but he shall baptize you
with the Holy Ghost.*

Mark 1:8

I had a cousin named John. He was known as somewhat
of an oddball, yet I knew him as an effective "voice" of the
Word. Called of God to prepare people for the coming
Messiah, he understood my calling whereas my brothers
did not.[82] His message was that the redemption of mankind
was near. I knew it was <u>very</u> near. I decided to travel to
where he was in the desert for a visit.

Kissing Mom good-bye, I headed out the door. "Make
sure you're home in time for the wedding," she added.

Approaching the Jordan River, I could see in the
distance the huge crowds gathered there. John was
baptizing scores of people while preaching the message
of repentance. A mixture of excitement and anticipation
welled up within me.

I was eager to begin teaching about the Kingdom of
God, that it was once again obtainable to all. The joy of
providing redemption to mankind was before me, and it

---

82   Neither did his brothers believe in him. John 7:5

was within my power to give. My goal: to provide a way for the lost to return to the Father.[83]

As I approached the crowd, suddenly all eyes turned in my direction. "Behold, the Lamb of God which takes away the sin of the world," John shouted as he pointed straight toward me.[84] As I came to the edge of the water he bowed his head in deference to my presence.

"John, I want to be baptized."

Surprised, he looked up. "Oh, no! I need to be baptized by you!"

"Allow it to happen. This is the Father's plan." Humbly, John gave in to my request and lowered me into the water—down, down, and up again.

As my head came up through the watery surface, I felt the Holy Spirit, like a dove, lightly land upon it. A powerful charge immediately ran through my body as a voice thundered from the heavens: "THIS IS MY BELOVED SON, IN WHOM I AM WELL PLEASED. LISTEN TO HIM."[85] Instantly I became aware of a potent sense of complete knowledge. Housed within my body of flesh resided the Spirit of God, which now directed me to go into the desert without delay.

I left without speaking a word to anyone.

Who am I? This question played over again in my mind as I pondered the evidence before me. I had an inner sense that I was not of this world, yet over the last thirty years I'd increasingly wondered about my place in humanity. That I was not only a Son of God, but The Lamb of God

---

[83]   I am the way, the truth and the Life. No man comes to the Father except by me. John 14:6

[84]   John 1:29

[85]   Matthew 17:5

was a thought that had been confirmed by John's recent proclamation.

All mankind were sons, in a sense;[86] sin caused them to be separated or "fallen," to be sure, but nevertheless still "sons" from a distinct past. In tracing my genealogy back to Adam it was written that Adam was "son of God." I was "the last Adam."[87] Adam had failed the test; I would not fail.

I required unhindered, uninterrupted time with my Heavenly Father to sort all this out. I had to get away from the cares and events of the world in order to hear his voice, to know it, and to not confuse it with any other spirit attempting to dilute the message.

Not one to casually make decisions, I measured each thought against the WORD. That I lived in a restricted human state meant I must weigh every decision for accuracy and signs of deception. I knew I must break through to unobstructed communication with my Heavenly Father.

Determined that nothing would deter me from accomplishing this task, I focused on what needed to be done. Fasting while praying was essential. I absolutely had to be of one mind with my Heavenly Father and eating would be a distraction from that goal.

I will not make a mistake. I will not fail.

As the days without food added up, my mission became crystal clear. I was to be the perfect, unspotted sacrificial lamb. I was to lay down my life for the salvation of the world.

---

86 Philippians 2:15; 1 John 3:2
87 See Luke 3:38 and 1 Cor 15:22

After forty days without food my body was on the verge of keto acidosis, a condition that would cause it to utilize the organs and muscles in order to sustain life. But I'd achieved perfect unity with HIM, a truly remarkable experience while in the carnal body of mankind. Now physically hungry beyond belief, the stones began to look like the delicious barley loves Mom would bake. The natural instinct of survival created a roaring desire to eat.

Sure enough, here came Lucifer disguised as an Angel of Light, tempting me to change the stones into bread. Finding me weak and emaciated, this fallen archangel thought it would be an easy task to convince me. He'd defeated Adam rather easily, I reminded myself, using the God-given basic instinct for food as a temptation.

But my spirit was strong, and I defeated the enemy with the power of THE WORD. More temptations followed, but I withstood each one. Finally, he gave up, leaving me alone.[88]

Lying down in a physically weakened state, a sense of joy washed over me. I had experienced using the sharp sword of the WORD to defeat evil. With this victory, everything was possible; I had no doubts that I would be able to redeem all of mankind through my death.

"Bravo!" I opened my eyes to see two angels kneeling beside me. "The Father sent this for you." In one outstretched hand was a tray containing a pitcher of ice water and two warm barley loaves. The other angel had a plate of fresh fruit peeled and ready to eat.

---

[88] For more details read Luke 4:1-13. Also the story is told in <u>Dark Stars of The Twilight</u>, copyright 2009 by Marilyn Olson.

Sitting up, I ate slowly as the two angels smiled and watched. It felt wonderful to be in the company of the holy—plus it was a most satisfying meal!

"Can we do anything for you? Wash your feet? Give a backrub?" I was worn out and happy to accept the generous offer. Finding a shaded area, I enjoyed the pampering.

Soon the heavenly messengers were gone and I was left with a heightened sense of well-being. I had successfully accessed the strength of the spoken WORD to defeat the enemy on his own turf.

I came away from the desert with clear direction, ready to take on the next level of my ministry. I would begin teaching in the Houses of Worship. Here the faithful gathered each week in obedience to God's law. It was the logical place to start.

Returning to Nazareth I entered the synagogue on the Sabbath day. When the appropriate time came, I stood up to read. The book of Isaiah was handed to me. I opened it and found the following passage:

"The Spirit of the Lord is upon me, because

1. he has anointed me to preach the gospel to the poor;
2. he has sent me to heal the brokenhearted,
3. to preach deliverance to the captives,
4. and recovering of sight to the blind,
5. to set at liberty them that are bruised,
6. to preach the acceptable year of the Lord."[89]

Closing the book, I sat down. Every eye was fastened on me. "Today this scripture is fulfilled."

Everyone there wondered at my words: *Isn't this Joseph's son?* Some were not too happy about my statement and threatened bodily harm, but I passed unseen through the middle of the crowd and headed to Capernaum. There, I did the same thing: I taught them on the Sabbath day.

I'm astonished at his teaching!

His word is with power!

From where did he get the authority to teach this way?

No one has ever spoken like he does.

It was time to organize my crew. Taking the humble from the earth, I gathered together the ones the Father had pointed out to me. Twelve men, each with different backgrounds and personalities, joined me in my mission. From the day I first requested their allegiance, I prayed for each one fervently. I knew I'd soon give my life for their salvation, and if for them, then also for the whole world.

---

[89] Isa 61:2

Chapter 16
The Wedding

Both Jesus and his disciples were called to the marriage.
John 2:2

The week before Judith's wedding Mom sent word for me to come home. I was fully aware of her desire that I not miss it. *Doesn't she understand the importance of my mission?* I had much teaching yet to convey.

"Son, all our friends will be there; everyone wants to see you."

"I've got some guys with me now, Mom."

"How many?"

"Twelve."

"Twelve? Why so many?" Mom was all-aflutter. My sisters required new garments; my brothers had yet to get out their best clothes and their worn-out sandals needed to be replaced with new ones.

I helped to get everything done to Mom's specifications. When all was ready, she sighed contentedly. "I have one more detail." With a twinkle in her eye, she presented to me a special gift: a new robe.

"This is for you, Jesus," she said softly. "It's quality, ideal for you." I looked at it, noticing the fine craftsmanship. It was unique, all right—no seam anywhere. The cloth had been woven into the garment with not a stitch added.

"Thank you, Mom." Lightly kissing her on the cheek, I put the robe on. "It's perfect."

"Just like you," she said softly. I would wear this robe for the next three years.

Dressed for the occasion, our family arrived at the wedding. The music put us all in a mood for dancing and we enjoyed the fun as we moved to the old Davidic melodies.

Not long into the festivities Mom approached me with a worried look as only a mother can give. "They're out of wine," she fretted. "Please do something!"

Mom, is this really what you want? My first miracle? To make wine for a wedding?

I didn't expect this, as there seemed to be much greater need around than providing wine. But I would honor my mother, for I realized some things were very important to women.

Giving her a reassuring look, I planned what to do. Fixing the problem wouldn't be hard: it was easy to divide and multiply molecules. Mom, her faith in me intact, told the servants to do whatever I said.

Instructing the help to fill up the water pots with water, I formulated the procedure in my mind and applied it to the water in the pots. Knowing the resulting wine was excellent, I enjoyed watching my mother's reaction as well as those of the guests. I winked at Mom as some asked the host: "Why did you save the best wine for last?"

The wedding crisis over, Mom looked at me with different eyes. She surmised, rightly so, that this first miracle of the wine was only the beginning.

She and Dad at last both accepted the fact that my ministry had begun.

Changing the water to wine was an easy task. Not only did I understand the chemical compositions of all elements, I also understood the power of true faith. With these tools I'd be able to access the formulas needed to correct the problems I found upon the earth.

But I was an oddity to my brothers. They didn't understand me at all, nor could they reason with any logic how I'd accomplished the miracle.

After the wedding, my disciples and I accompanied my family to Capernaum for a few days. Since the Passover was near, I wanted to continue on to the temple in Jerusalem to celebrate it.

The long, steep climb to the city was invigorating. Each step brought me closer to my Father's House. The time for which I had spent a lifetime of preparation, had finally come.

With the advent of the feast day of Passover, I was where I wanted to be: in Jerusalem teaching truths to God's people. *There are many who'll believe my words once they witness the miracles.*

Arriving at the noisy courtyard was a shock back to reality. It had deteriorated into a marketplace! Hawkers were yelling, frightened sheep and oxen were making terrible noises. Doves and other birds were messing up the grounds. Observing this, a determination stirred within me. These merchants had made my Father's house into a den of thieves! Quickly fashioning a whip of small cords, I drove them all out of the area: the sheep, birds and oxen scattered as I turned over the tables and dumped the money onto the ground.

"Take these things away. Don't make my Father's house a place of merchandise."

Skulking before me, the moneychangers crept away. As I watched them, I realized where they were headed: to the area of the temple where the Pharisees gathered for their debates.

Good. As men known for their devout attention to the law they should feel the same way I do about it!

Expecting the Pharisees to support the cleansing of the temple grounds was more of a wishful thought. As they approached me, I perceived they'd not only given permission to sell livestock in the courtyard, but would also receive a cut from the profits.

With one glance I instantly knew the inner characters of the seven men who approached me:[90] *Three complete hypocrites, two scholars who are full of pride and arrogance, a* wolf *in sheep's clothing, and . . . there's one who actually wants to serve God. All are hiding secret sins.*

"What sign do you give to prove you have the authority to do this?" asked one revered teacher of the law.

"Destroy this temple, and in three days I'll raise it up."

"Forty-six years it took to build this, and you can rebuild it in three days?"

I was more amazed at their lack of knowledge than of their lack of faith. These renowned scholars hadn't a clue that I was speaking about my own body. Many of them at this time, however, were interested in me because of the miracles I performed. Yet I didn't commit to them because I could see the bias in their hearts.[91]

---

[90] John 2:24
[91] John 2:25

Chapter 17

The Pharisees

Beware of the leaven of the Pharisees.

Matt 16:6

Dogmatic at times, the Pharisees had replaced the joy of attainable salvation with a list of do's and don'ts, making life hard and tedious for those who wanted to serve God. I had to break the yoke the teachers of the law had not only put on God's people, but onto themselves as well.

Nicodemus was one of these. Though misguided, he had a genuine thirst for knowing the truth of the scriptures. He was one of the Pharisees who took notice of the miracles I did in the temple. As a result he wanted to secretly meet with me.

"The counselor Joseph owns a garden nearby," he whispered after most of the group of Pharisees had left. "Meet me tonight."

"I'll see you there," I whispered back with a smile, knowing he was breaking out of the mold the rest were entrenched in.

As soon as I entered Joseph's garden, I knew the place would have a special significance for me. There were olive trees with an oil press at one end. Nearby was a new tomb where two gravesites were being carved out of the rock. A peaceful place, the sounds of chirping birds and the sweet smell of flowers permeated the air. Located a short distance from the Sheep Gate and just out of hearing range from the noise that resonated from the city, it was a perfect place to pray.

Arriving late in the night, I perceived that Nicodemus was honest and sincere in his questions. He'd studied the law for the right reasons: he wanted to be right with Jehovah.[92]

"I know you're from God, for no man can do the miracles you do unless God is with him," he began.

"You must be born again to enter the Kingdom of God." With that startling statement, I'd gotten his attention.

"How can a man be born when he's old?" Though a doctor of the law, he didn't understand what I meant. I was happy to explain it to him.

"Mankind on Earth gives birth to human bodies; but it's the Spirit that births our spirits into the Kingdom."[93]

"How can this be?"

"I came down from Heaven to be lifted up from the earth in death. Anyone who believes in me will have eternal life. God loved the world so much that he gave me, his Son, to the world. He that believes on me is not condemned, but he that doesn't believe is already condemned.[94]

God's Light has come into the world, but men love darkness rather than light because of their evil deeds. He that

---

[92] Jehovah is a Hebrew name for God. Ps 83:18
[93] That which is born of the flesh is flesh, but that which is born of the sprit is spirit. John 3:6
[94] He stays in his present lost state due to Lucifer's current authority over him.

lives by truth is happy to come to the light, unashamed of what he does. Those that do evil try to stay in the dark."[95]

I could tell Nicodemus was listening. Intelligent, he understood the concepts I imparted to him. *He's the one who'll speak truth to his peers.*[96]

The next morning as my disciples and I traveled back to Judea we came to a place where there was a lot of water. We stopped to baptize the new believers who followed us there. At the same time my cousin John was baptizing new believers near the town of Salim.

As soon as we entered the water, the Pharisees arrived with their jealousies, manipulations and misguided judgments. Their motivation was obvious: they wanted to cause trouble. After the last baptism was over, they hurried to Salim where John was working, hoping to cause jealousy with the news that my disciples had baptized more believers than he had. But John surprised them with his answer: "He must increase while I must decrease." [97]

True workers in the Kingdom aren't in competition with each other. They work together, encouraging, complementing, and appreciating each one's effort.

I didn't receive any encouragement from the Pharisees.

As we commenced walking to Judea we passed through a little village in Samaria named Sychar. It was about noon when we reached Jacob's well at the city's outskirts.

Sitting down in a shady spot, I instructed my men to go into the city to buy some lunch. Having been up late the night before with Nicodemus, I was tired and wanted to rest.

---

[95] Text taken from John 3
[96] John 7:50-51. See also John 19:39.
[97] John 3:30

Soon a young woman came to draw water from the well. Glancing at me sideways with a somewhat flirtatious look, I knew instantly not only what she was thinking, but her total past history. This woman was miserable, lonely, and had poor self-esteem.

I asked her: "Will you give me a drink?"

"How is it that you, being a Jew asks a drink of me, a Samaritan woman?"

"If you knew the gift of God and who it is that's asking you, you'd ask me instead for living water."

"Mister, you don't have anything with which to draw water and the well is deep. From where would you get this "living water"? Are you greater than our ancestor Jacob who gave us this well in the first place?"

"Whoever drinks this water will get thirsty again, but whoever drinks the water I give will never get thirsty. It will be like a well of water bubbling within him, springing up into everlasting life."

"All right then. Give me this water so I won't ever have to come here again."

"Go get your husband and come back."

"I have no husband."

"That's right, for you've had five husbands, and the man you now have is not your husband.

She froze, shocked I'd so perfectly nailed her situation. She decided to change tactics; "I perceive you're a prophet . . . okay, where do we worship? Our fathers worshipped here, but your people say it's got to be in Jerusalem."

"God is a Spirit. He searches for those anywhere who will worship him in spirit and in truth."

"When the Messiah comes he'll tell us everything."

"I am He."

A flush of recognition suddenly came over her delicate features. She recognized the truth, and its revelation wiped out her hidden resistance to it.

Embracing the news, she went through the village exclaiming about her encounter with me. "He told me everything I've ever done," she excitedly proclaimed.[98]

Imparting truth to the spiritually hungry gave me such tremendous satisfaction that it was just like eating a big meal! My disciples, who'd returned by now with food, didn't understand why I was no longer hungry.

There were many new believers from Sychar because of this incident. We stayed two more days to teach them about Kingdom living. Many others also believed during our stay there. It was heartening to see how God's truths satisfied those who were hungry for His Word. "We've heard him ourselves and know that this is indeed the Christ, the Savior of the world."

Experiencing much joy at their newfound hope, we left the new believers in Samaria to continue our journey to Judea. Just before arriving at our destination, I was approached by a nobleman whose son was sick. Having no doubt in his mind as to what I'd do, he asked me to heal his son.

"If you don't come, he'll die," was his humble appeal. In this father's heart was genuine love. I felt his concern; I would not leave him without helping the situation.

"Your son now lives," I stated simply.[99] His faith was strong, so it was an easy task for me to speak the WORD and thereby remove the virus from the child's body.

---

[98]   Story from John 4
[99]   John 4:50

As the nobleman went home, his servants came rushing up to him with the happy news that his son had suddenly become well.

"When?" he asked. The answer revealed it was the exact moment I told him his son was healed. This was my second miracle in Cana. Word about it spread quickly.

Chapter 18

Work for the Kingdom

Unless your righteousness exceeds that of the scribes and Pharisees, you shall not enter the Kingdom of Heaven.

Matt 5:20

After our visit in Judea, we returned to Jerusalem for the second feast.[100] Arriving at the city we found a good place to rest near the Sheep Gate. Close by was the pool of Siloam; people were camped everywhere, hoping the water would heal them.

There was among them a man who'd been sick many years. Watching him, I knew he had strong faith.

"Do you want to be healed?"

"I move too slowly. Once the waters move others always beat me to it. I've no one to help me."

"Pick up your bed and walk." As the meaning of my words dawned on him, I saw belief arise in his heart. He picked up his bed and was instantly healed.

---

[100] The chronological order is taken from the book of John. John indicated that there were many more events that took place than he reported. See John 21:25

Grinning from ear to ear, he soon headed to the temple. His desire was to worship God within its doors, something he'd not been able to do for the last thirty-eight years.

The Pharisees were perplexed. They knew the man had been sick a long time—they'd seen him daily sitting outside the gates of Jerusalem. Instead of being happy that God had healed him, however, they immediately began a harassment campaign. Their jealousy inspired a search for something for which they could accuse me to my audience. "He can't be of God. He forced this man to work on the Sabbath day by ordering him to carry his bed. We know this man is a sinner!"

Disappointed but not surprised, I made mental notes:

Pharisees:
1. criticized rather than encouraged
2. were angry that believers followed me
3. never smiled at or complimented me on anything
4. were unhappy with my wise answers to them
5. were enraged that God confirmed my WORD with healings and miracles

Conclusion: They were jealous of me in the same way that Cain was jealous of Abel. Unless their hearts changed, murder would be their next step.

The fact that they knew I saw their motivations escalated the troubling aspect of animosity the Pharisees had towards me. One would have expected these wise teachers from the temple to confirm the WORD as they recognized its truths. Their accusing attitude, however, wouldn't deter me from my mission. I determined to move forward no matter what they said.

Looking one of them squarely in the face I stated, "My Father works here, and so do I." [101]

Angered that I'd not only "broken the Sabbath" but now said that God was my Father, they looked for ways to cause my death.

I knew what was in their hearts. Boldly I looked at another of the pompous crowd. "Why do you want to kill me?"

How does he know this? "You're crazy! Who wants to kill you?"

"The Father raises up the dead, and gives them life. So I'll raise up who I will. I'm telling you these things so that you can be saved. Search the scriptures—you say you believe in them. When you do you'll see that Moses himself testified of me.

The Son can do nothing of himself, but only what he sees the Father doing. The time is almost here when the dead of the earth will hear the voice of the Son of God and in so doing, shall live."[102]

I'm offering life to those who want to kill me.

Kingdom Truths

After my discussion with the Pharisees we left for Judea; I planned to celebrate the Feast of Passover there with my family. Leaving Jerusalem, we came to the Sea of Galilee. By now word had spread, and a huge crowd followed me everywhere, giving me no privacy at all. The people were like sheep needing a shepherd. Teaching them Kingdom concepts was my passion.

---

[101] John 5:17
[102] John 5:25.

A flower-strewn hill was nearby—a perfect place to teach and be heard. I walked up the grassy hill and sat down with my disciples.

As the huge crowd gathered on the hill below me, I began the teaching.

1. Happy are the humble, for theirs is the Kingdom of Heaven.
2. Happy are they that mourn, for they'll be comforted.
3. Happy are the meek for they'll inherit the earth.
4. Happy are those who hunger and thirst after righteousness, for they'll be filled.
5. Happy are the merciful, for they'll receive mercy.
6. Happy are the pure in heart, for they'll see God.
7. Happy are the peacemakers, for they'll be known as the children of God.
8. Happy are those who are persecuted because of their commitment to righteousness, for theirs is the Kingdom of Heaven.

"When people insult and bully you, and say all kinds of false things about you for my sake, be ecstatically happy, for you'll have a great reward in Heaven. You're on the same level with the prophets who were mistreated before you."

"You're the salt of the earth. You are the light of the world. Let your light shine before others that they may see your good deeds and glorify your Father in Heaven."

"Give to others in need. Love your enemies. Bless them that curse you, be kind to the ones who hate you, and pray for those who treat you wrongly."

"Perfection is the goal. Be as perfect as is your Father in Heaven."[103]

The crowd listened, astonished at my teaching. They'd not understood that giving would make them happier than taking[104] —that God himself supplies the needs as well as blesses those who are generous to others.[105]

After the teaching was over I realized many of the people hadn't eaten all day. Turning to Phillip I asked "Where can we buy enough food for them?" Though already knowing what I was going to do, I wanted to see if Phillip had been listening to what I'd been saying.

"We don't have enough money to feed this crowd!" he exclaimed.

"There's a boy here who has five barley loaves and two small fish," Peter remarked, "but they're a drop in the bucket compared to what we need."

"Tell everyone to sit down."

I took the loaves, using the same principle of multiplication I'd used before with the wine. After giving thanks, I broke off pieces of bread into the baskets and handed them to the disciples to pass around. After everyone was fully satisfied, there were twelve basketsful of bread left.

Seeing this miracle, the crowd wanted to make me their king right then and there. Talk about shortcuts! I firmly declined the offer, knowing that this wasn't the right time.

Now both physically and spiritually full, the crowd gradually thinned as the people returned home. Feeling an immediate need for undistracted communication with my

---

[103]   Text taken from Matthew 5
[104]   Acts 20:35
[105]   See Mal.3:10 Luke 6:38

FATHER, I quietly hiked to the top of the mountain while the rest of the disciples took the boat across the lake.

Praying was energizing as I reconnected to my SOURCE of strength; hearing my Father's guiding voice brought a refreshing to my spirit. Soon the night stars were the only light on the mountaintop.

Down below I could hear the wind whipping the waves on the water. I sensed that my disciples were frightened as they battled the tempest in the black of the night. *I must go to them.*

Moving at lightening speed I ran down the mountain and stepped onto the surface of the water. Buoyed up by the rising and falling waves, I jumped across the gullies as I hurried along.

Approaching the ship I heard some yell, "It's a ghost!"

"Don't be afraid," I shouted back. "It's me, Jesus." Entering the boat, I immediately transported it to shore.

The next day the crowds were perplexed as to how I'd crossed the sea; I didn't see a need to explain it to them. Instead, I told them something they didn't expect: "I'm the Bread of life, the living bread that came down from Heaven. If anyone eats my flesh and drinks my blood he'll live forever. I'll give my body to give life to the world."

They had questions. "This is a difficult concept. Who can believe it?"

"Does this bother you? The words I speak are spiritual and give life to the spirit. But some of you don't believe."[106]

---

[106]   John 6:48-64

Not understanding, most of the new disciples left, unwilling to follow me anymore. "Will you also leave?" I asked the twelve.

Peter answered for the group: "To whom shall we go? You alone have the words of eternal life. You're the Christ, the Son of the living God."

I've chosen you twelve, yet one is a devil.

This had been a tough day.

Chapter 19

Danger in Jerusalem

—Neither did his brothers believe in him.

John 7:5

After this event, I avoided the areas where the most dangerous Jewish fanatics gathered. They were like a pack of wolves, eager to tear me to pieces. I decided to keep a low profile, for I knew it wasn't yet time for me to die.

Not understanding the risk, my brother Joses urged me, "Come to the feast in Judea, as planned."

"It's too dangerous for me to be seen right now."

"Nobody sneaks around secretly if they want to be openly noticed," added brother James. "If you're going to do these miracles, then proudly show yourself to the world."

My brothers don't believe in me either.

"The world doesn't hate you—only me, because I expose its evil conduct. Go up to this feast by yourselves. The timing may be right for you, but it's not for me."[107]

At this celebration I was the subject of most conversations. Some said I was a good teacher, others alleged that I "deceive the people." But the ones who were for me spoke guardedly for fear of reprisals from the Jewish leaders.

---

[107] John 7:7

"How is this man so highly knowledgeable, having never been educated?" This was a question repeated so often that when I finally did show up at the feast, I answered it.

"My doctrine isn't mine, but HIS that sent me. Anyone who lives in harmony with HIS will knows if this doctrine is from God or birthed from my own skill and knowledge."

"Is anyone thirsty? Come to me and drink; if you believe, living water will flow out of your bellies."[108]

The people were curious: "Do the rulers know this is the Christ? He's speaking openly in the temple, yet they don't stop him. What do they know that we don't?"

The Pharisees had their own opinions: *Jesus hasn't earned the right to do what he does. God, is this fair? I've dedicated my life to studying the scriptures, yet I can't heal anyone.*

Why him? Why not me?

Quickly calling a meeting, the leaders got together to look for ways to discredit me. "Does God break his own rules and heal on the Sabbath?"

"Aha!"

"We've got him!"

"He quotes scripture . . . let's use the Law against him!"

Turning to the officer present, one leader spoke sharply: "Why haven't you taken him in already?"

"No one has ever before spoken like this."

"Are you also deceived?"

Another chimed in, "We know from where the real Christ will come. The scriptures plainly tell us he'll come from Bethlehem. But listen . . . ." the teacher gloated proudly with the information he was about to impart; "We know for a fact that this man comes from Galilee, not Bethlehem."

---

[108] Healing properties would be in any of Jesus' bodily fluids.

"There's your proof, right there in black and white. This man is definitely not the Christ."

Finally Nicodemus spoke up "Does our law judge anyone before it hears the other side?"

"Are you from Galilee as well? Search the prophecies. No prophet comes from this town." The teachers were at odds.

"We'll test him."[109]

---

[109] Text from John 7.

Chapter 20

Wise Answers

—The spirit of the Lord shall rest upon him, the spirit of wisdom—

Isaiah 11:2

After a night of prayer on the Mount of Olives, I returned to the temple early the next morning. As soon as I was noticed, the people ran toward me, wanting me to teach them again. The scribes and Pharisees arrived also, smugly bringing with them a disheveled-appearing young woman.

"Master, this woman was caught in the very act of committing adultery. According to the law Moses gave us, she's to be stoned . . . but what do you say?"

I glanced at the woman and instantly knew her heart. In looking for affection, she'd given herself to someone who didn't love her. When their adultery was exposed, he quickly turned against her.

I felt her sorrow, her absolute grief and suicidal thoughts. Betrayed and humiliated, she was brokenhearted. Glancing up momentarily I looked at each of the leaders. As I focused on their hearts they began to fidget uncomfortably.

He's looking right through me. Does he know about my secret addiction?

"He who is sinless among you, let him throw the first stone." Stooping down, I wrote words in the dust with my finger, paying no attention to the guilty, self-righteous crowd. One by one they left until only the woman remained.

"Where'd they go? Didn't anyone stay here to condemn you?"

"No one."

"I don't condemn you either. Go home, and don't sin any more."

Through a face wet with tears, she smiled her thanks. Scampering off she stopped just once to glance back at me. As she did, I perceived what was in her mind. Her thoughts were these: *Never in my life have I felt so valued and loved.*

Returning the smile, I proceeded to the treasury room of the temple to begin my teaching session. Though now once again amongst the most dangerous of the religious Jews, FATHER assured me I'd be safe; it wasn't yet time to lay down my life.

I looked over the small band of scholars and began to speak: "I'm the light of the world. He who follows me will no longer walk in darkness, but will have the light of life."

"Aha! Because you bear record of yourself, your record isn't true."

"Your law states that the testimony of two witnesses confirms a fact as true. I'm one witness and the Father that sent me is the other witness."

"Where is your Father?"

"If you really knew me, you would also know my Father. I'm not from this world; but I know from where I came and where I'm going."

"Where are you going?"

"You're from beneath the earth, I'm from above. If you don't believe in me, you'll die in your sins and not be able to join me."

"Who are you?"

"When you've lifted me up, you'll know that I AM HE; I do nothing by myself, but only the things which please my Father."

After hearing this, many of the Jews believed in me. Speaking softly, I explained: "If you continue absorbing my WORD into your lives, you will truly become my disciples. Knowing the truth will make you free."

"We, as Abraham's descendants, were never in bondage. What do you mean 'you'll be free'?"

"Whoever commits sin is its servant."

Does he know about my addictions and secret sins?

"If the SON makes you free, than you're truly free from sin's addictions."

Other leaders took offense, trying to trip me up, calling me a "Samaritan" and accusing me of hosting a devil.

"If anyone keeps my sayings, he'll never see death. Believe me, your father Abraham was glad when he saw my day." *He understood what it took for God to sacrifice his Son to save others.*

"You're not even fifty years old, yet you claim to have seen Abraham?"

"Before Abraham was, I AM."

Enraged at my words, some again attempted to stone me. But I hid as I left the treasury room by passing right through the center of the group.

Exiting the temple, I noticed a blind man sitting nearby, who'd been blind from birth. My disciples had a question about him: "Who sinned, himself or his parents?"

"Neither. The works of God will be noticeable through this man." *My saliva has the same healing DNA as my blood.* Spitting on the ground I picked up the resulting mud, placing some on each eye.

"Go wash in the pool of Siloam." The man did as I asked.

"I can see!" he shouted as he skipped around the courtyard. Happy for him, the crowd clapped and cheered as he continued his exuberant dance.

Healing the man born blind, however, caused certain of the Pharisees to become very unhappy. These jealous ones determined that God was making a mistake by validating my message with miracles! There was a division among the leaders.

"He is the Christ"

"He is a prophet."

"He has a devil and is mad. Why listen to him?"

"These are not the words of him that has a devil. Can a devil open the eyes of the blind?"

Return to Jerusalem

It was winter when I returned to Jerusalem to celebrate the Feast of Dedication. Arriving early, I entered the temple through Solomon's porch.

"Isn't this the man they're trying to kill? Yet he again preaches openly in the temple. Do the rulers indeed know that this is the Christ?"

Soon the teachers of the law surrounded me. "How long will you keep us in the dark? If you're Christ, tell us plainly."

"I told you, and you didn't believe me. The works I do in my Father's name, they speak for me.

They still don't believe who I am. I'll refer to one of their favorite topics of discussion: David's shepherd analogy.

"I'm the Good Shepherd who's willing to give his life for the sheep. A hired hand runs away when he sees danger approaching because he doesn't care for the sheep. But my sheep know me, and I know them just as the Father knows me and I know him. Because I willingly give my life for the sheep, the Father loves me. He's given me the power to lay down my life, as well as to take it up again."

"Those who are mine will believe I came from the Father. I'm able to give them eternal life so that they never die. Those who don't believe me are not mine. My Father and I are one."[110]

---

[110] Text taken from John 10, whole chapter.

We've got him. He put himself equal with God. "This is blasphemy!" Eagerly they took up stones to stone me.

"For which of my good works do you kill me?" I calmly asked.

"You, a man, make yourself equal with God."

"Isn't it written in your law 'You are gods'? Do you say that I blaspheme because I told you I am the Son of God? If I don't do my Father's job, then don't believe me. But if I do, then know and believe that the Father's in me and I'm in HIM."

Angered at my logic, they responded by again trying to grab and kill me, but I escaped, traveling quickly to the place where John first baptized beyond Jordan. Though saddened at the state of the Pharisees, I was encouraged by the believers who came to see me.

While there, many others came to understand and accept the truth. Being able to perceive what was in their hearts affected the way I dealt with each one. As usual, I had perfect clarity.

Chapter 21

Healings

To you that fear my name shall the Sun of righteousness arise with healing in his wings;

Malachi 4:2

The group in the archive room watched in fascination as three years of ministry flew by. Every day Jesus taught about Kingdom living; every day his words gave purpose to those with no hope. Explaining how God's law was more than a set of harsh rules, he encapsulated it in one sentence: "Love God and love each other."

Defining love as giving, sharing, praying, encouraging, forgiving, being patient and believing in each other, his premise that "God is Love" went against the attitude of legalism into which Jewish law had evolved.[111] The stories Jesus told to illustrate his teachings were simple, yet profound in their message. People could relate to them on a grass roots level.

The more Jesus preached, however, the more the Pharisees became outraged. "Who does he think he is?" they fumed privately. Yet they were afraid of the people who believed in Him, for they couldn't deny his many marvelous

---

[111]   1 John 4:8; 16

miracles. He cured those who were sick, restored to health the blind and lame, cast out devils and raised the dead.

Still, the spirit of Cain persisted amongst the religious leaders. They continually questioned God: *Why Him? Why not us?* They refused to believe the answer, that Jesus was the Messiah for whom they'd been waiting. God had already confirmed his WORD with miracles. Why would they not humble themselves to simply believe it?

Jealousy has neither reason nor logic to it. Instead of seeking to learn God's true ways, the religious leaders were determined to make God bless them within the context of their misguided understanding. *After all, we've given our lives for service to the temple. We've spent hours studying; we know all the right answers to every question.* Their delusional determination caused them to miss the point in the same way Cain missed the point: they harbored a proud refusal to learn from the one who got it right.

It isn't that God loves one more than another. There's a process that has to be followed in order to fulfill the requirements for salvation. For Cain, a sacrificial lamb had to be used rather than vegetables and fruit. For the Pharisees, their manipulative lies as well as their demanding set of rules had to be exposed to the light of truth in order for their hearts to change. Without repentance their jealousy would be deadly.

Jesus, who'd first started his ministry in the synagogues, now taught in fields, by lakes and on mountain slopes. These open places were better suited to accommodate his huge following, for even the largest synagogues were not big enough to hold the burgeoning crowds.

The friends in the archive room watched as Jesus healed the sick while the Pharisees, envious of his success, seethed with anger. The vehement outrage and manipulative behavior of the leaders did little to stop Jesus from continuing his mission. His Word, sharp as a Two-Edged Sword, would accurately divide the proverbial sheep from the goats. Starting in Jerusalem, the powerful truth would gradually spread throughout the entire world.

Though busy with the crowds that followed him, Jesus still made it a priority to mentor his twelve disciples. Calling them "friends," he showed by example what it meant to be one.

But even with his loving attention the heart of one of them remained unchanged. Judas loved money more than God; in exchange for riches he schemed with the Pharisees to betray Jesus. Aware of his plot, Jesus knew this disciple would not only condemn himself, but also be forever lost.[112]

Sensing that the time of betrayal was near, Jesus went to pray in the garden owned by counselor Joseph. Here, carved right into the rocky knoll was a new tomb in the final stages of construction. Only one of the two gravesites had been completed. Jesus perceived that this sepulcher would soon be his own burial chamber.

---

[112]   Jesus knew this from the beginning. See John 6:64

Chapter 22
Riding into Jerusalem

Rejoice greatly, O daughter of Zion; shout, O daughter of Jerusalem: your King comes to you: he is just, and having salvation; lowly, and riding upon the foal of a donkey.
Zechariah 9:9

It was Passover time. Jesus recognized that this seasonal feast was a shadow of his impending death. *In the same way the innocent lamb's blood dripped from the doorposts in Egypt, my blood will drip to the ground. Only then will the ransom for every human be paid for in full.* The pending event was very close; he was restless to complete the task.

His instructions were clearly laid out by his ever-present Heavenly Father as he guided his every move. He was to enter into Jerusalem for the last time, but not as a baby or young boy of twelve—not even to cleanse the temple or to teach in it. It was to be a triumphal entry, a foreshadowing of the future when he would return as a victorious king to rule the whole earth.

Jesus climbed the hill overlooking Jerusalem, his heart breaking with grief. As he looked over the city, he saw not only the present beautiful temple, but also its future as it lay in ruins. A symbol of hatred would be prominently placed where the beautiful courtyard had once been.[113]

Anguished, he watched future generations make the journey to the remaining temple wall to pray only to be accosted by another jealous brother who refused to do things God's way: Ishmael.[114]

Ishmael's apostate descendants would boldly build on the temple's very grounds in an attempt to prevent God's true followers from worshiping him. Their noisy "call to prayer" would be a counterfeit to the genuine methods the Father had put forth. Not only in Jerusalem, but in synagogues and churches all over the world, this dangerous religion would erect their towers in an earsplitting attempt to dominate and control. Whereas Jesus taught love, this counterfeit religion would teach hate. While God's true followers build and restore, the counterfeit religion would teach their followers to kill and destroy.

The motivation was simple: Cain's jealousy of Abel was repeated in a nation that felt rejected by God. Rather than learning from the brother who got it right, they would demand recognition for their misguided religious acts.

Look how holy we are! See, we pray five times a day—do you notice? Never do we allow 'sin' in any form; we control our people through rules and terror. We kill anyone, even daughters and sons if they don't follow our religion. You've got to take notice! See how dedicated we are?

Jesus saw it all, and it made him weep.

---

[113] Mark 13:14. See also Daniel 12:11 (One definition of the word "abomination" is "hatred.")

[114] See Gal 4:22-30, specifically verse 29.

"Oh Jerusalem, Jerusalem, you who kill the prophets. How I would have gathered you under my wing and protected you, but you refused!"

Later as he rode into Jerusalem on a young donkey's colt, the people shouted, "Hosanna, blessed is the King of Israel that comes in the name of the Lord!"[115] It was a moment that would be noted and remembered, for Jesus would come again when the last day of testing was over and the Thousand-Year Reign had begun.

Eating supper that evening for the last time with his disciples, Jesus told them again how his body and blood must be consumed for salvation. By breaking the bread with his hands, and drinking from the communal cup, Jesus left microscopic amounts of his own DNA in the food and drink. Still not really understanding how this would pay their ransom, the disciples ate the bread and wine as a token of their faith in His redemptive plan.

Jesus understood. "I am come a light into the world. Whoever believes on me will not live in darkness."[116]

Jesus had one more task to do that night: wash his disciples' feet. "If I, being your Lord wash your feet, you also ought to wash each other's feet." As he lovingly completed this lowly task, his actions imprinted the scene into their souls.

The Messiah is taking a servant's role. This concept is very different from the world's way of thinking.

Jesus spoke again. "I'm going away, but my Father will send the Comforter to continue to teach you all things."

"Where are you going?" asked Peter.

---

[115] John 12:13
[116] John 12:46

"Speak plainly to us," they all begged. "What's going to happen?"

"Don't be troubled; in my Father's house are many mansions. I'm going to prepare your eternal home for your arrival."

With that statement, Jesus gave his final words of wisdom to his disciples. Revealing many details about future events, he ended his conversation with the following words: "I'm leaving my peace with you. Though the prince of this world is coming, he has nothing on me; he wasn't able to cause me to sin in any way."

"The incidents about to take place will occur so the world will know I love the Father. I'll do everything HE requires me to do."

"Pray with me. My time has come."[117]

---

[117]   John 14:26-31

Chapter 23

It is Finished!

Behold the Lamb of God, which takes away the sin of the world.

John 1:29

Jesus and his twelve disciples left for the garden. Soon Jesus was praying so intensely that his sweat turned bloody as it ran down his face.

"Father, if possible, let this cup pass from me. Yet not my will, but yours be done." *If the mission can't be completed unless I go through this, then I'll do it. It's why I came here—to give myself as a sacrifice.* Knowing he would soon be reunited with his Father, he determined to see the mission accomplished to the tiniest detail.

The plan was this: Death would come after suffering at the hands of those who should have welcomed him. He would then enter the Pit to release the long held captives and bring them to the light where they would be free from the cursed power of darkness.

Soon Judas arrived. With him were the misguided religious leaders who were intent on murder. Approaching Jesus, Judas wondered at the sweaty, bloody face. Kissing him on the cheek, Judas tasted saltiness as Jesus' sweat and blood with its pure DNA entered his mouth; inevitably he swallowed a miniscule amount of the mixture. Unaware, he'd just tasted from the forbidden Tree of Life. His spirit would now live forever in its present sinful state.

Jesus was taken to Pilate's palace where he was mocked, tried, whipped., convicted, and sentenced to death. Not saying a word during the torture, he was as a lamb being led to the slaughterhouse.

Jesus

Unknown to the rest of the world, I went willingly, for I knew this was the process needed in order to redeem mankind. Unlike Cain who wanted the method changed and was bitter that he had no power to change it, I knew that this course of action was not mine to change. I had to fit into the pre-determined plan in order to accomplish its purpose.

The whipping, the abuse—it was painful, but the presence of MY FATHER made it bearable. Surely God would not ask anything that wasn't do-able, and I firmly resolved to endure to the end.

After my conviction I was forced to carry a heavy wooden cross through the streets of Jerusalem. The weight was heavy, and rubbed against my open wounds. More than that, I knew I would soon bear unspeakable agony upon it.

At length we arrived at the crucifixion site. Nearby was a rocky hill that resembled the face of a skull. Also close by was the unfinished tomb.

Here is where I'll give up my life.

My comfort was this: My Father was with me; HE would be with me with every phase of this horrendous death.

The nails were pounded in without mercy. *So much pain!* Pain was created by the evil side and used extensively in its hierarchy. In the flesh, mankind was designed to avoid pain at all costs. Yet the Spirit is stronger than the flesh, and I determined to succeed in finishing my task. Unimaginable joy would soon be mine once salvation for all was achieved through my death.

The soldiers hammered the nails into my wrists, careful to keep their clothing away from the blood that was dripping. Picking up my clothing, they divided the pieces between them. Finding that my robe was seamless and not wanting to tear it up, they played a game of lots to see who would win the prize. My mother, eyes streaming with tears, watched the gambling activity.

My head ached with the pounding; the pain was incredible as they placed the cross in an upright position, but my Father constantly comforted me. He had been there with me at the mock of a trial with every answer I gave to the chief priests; he was also there when I remained silent. Every word out of my mouth was only a repeat of what the Father whispered into my ear. When there was no whisper, I didn't speak.[118]

The agony of trying to breathe while lifting up my battered body on the cross took superhuman strength. With a steady stream of blood oozing out, my body became weaker. Still my compassion was for the thieves on each side of me who were moaning and cursing in agony. It was obvious that neither of them had prepared their souls for this moment. One spoke: "If you're truly the Messiah, save yourself and us."

The other one had a different attitude: "Aren't you afraid? We're all in the same boat. We got what we deserved, but he's done nothing wrong." Turning his head toward

---

[118] John 8:26. One of many references where Jesus says he speaks only what he hears from his Father.

me he spoke haltingly between agonized breaths: "Lord, remember me when you come into your Kingdom."

I answered with words of truth, comforting the dying man: "Today you'll be with me in Paradise." *I offered them both eternal life. One received it, the other rejected it.*

Through my pain I watched the crowd that gathered. If only they knew to believe in me! *They don't understand how short their lives are; they'll return to the Pit unless they put their trust in me. Oh, that they'd turn from deception and embrace the truth before it's too late!*

I uttered one last prayer for the world: "Father, forgive them for they don't know what they're doing!" I cried out to save even the ones causing my agony.

Hours passed. Suddenly the earth grew dark. I found myself alone. The Father's presence was gone. *What's happening? Is this part of the plan?* "FATHER, WHY HAVE YOU ABANDONED ME?" My cry thundered out over the crowd. I knew I could call ten thousand angels—oh, the thought did cross my mind. Yet my determination was so strong, pure and focused that the fleeting thought had nowhere to take root.

I will persevere no matter what!

Though I didn't understand why I was on my own, it didn't change my commitment. *I'll die, then, alone.* Such was my drive to complete with my death the redemption of mankind. *I'll not fail, not even in the last moments of my human life.*

"IT IS FINISHED!"

One more agonizing moment, and I felt my spirit leave my body. Though the separation from my Father was more than the worst feeling of loneliness imaginable, my obedience conquered my emotions. The atonement was complete. The dying was over and the price of redemption had been paid. I felt a rush of victorious joy, for I had finished everything the Father had required of me.

Elated in knowing I'd broken Lucifer's grip of evil, I watched momentarily as John took my mother's arm and tenderly helped her walk to his house. Yes, she would be lovingly taken care of by him for the rest of her days. I'd handpicked him for that purpose as his gentle personality and strong faith would be an encouragement to her in these days of sorrow.

Warm feelings swept over me as I silently said good-bye to the woman who'd given me birth. She would be honored and loved by millions in ages to come.

As my spirit began to soar in the air, I noticed my body, still on the cross, bloodied and bruised. Yes, I had taken a beating . . . my blood was now gushing to the ground due to a post-mortem pierce of a sword. But because I'd kept my blood pure from sin, it would never deteriorate. Its healing powers would be forever planted in the world of man, spreading through the air and soil as its molecules separated into billions of cells. These particles in turn would eventually permeate every part of the earth and water.

My blood also soaked well into the rocky soil, running down the cracked basalt like a funnel—down, down, until it dripped onto the very mercy seat of the Ark of the Covenant hidden long ago in a cavern beneath the rock.[119]

---

[119] The entrance to Jeremiah's cave is located just a few feet from the place of the skull. The Ark of the Covenant was hidden many years before during Israel's captivity. There is some indication that deep within this cave is the place where it was recently found. The cave entrance, as of today, has been blocked off and is now inaccessible to the general public. See also www.CovenantKeepers.co.uk for fascinating information.

Chapter 24

Release the Prisoners!

To bring out the prisoners from the prison, and them that sit in darkness out of the prison house.

Isa 42:7

I had work to do. Gathering my wits about me, I mentally prepared for the task at hand. I knew where the gates were . . . FATHER had prepared me well. Entering into the tunnel, I achieved lightening speeds available only to Deity. As I made my entrance into the Pit, an earthquake rocked the chambers. I brought light into this world of darkness, light that could never again be quenched.

"Release the Prisoners!" I shouted. The inhabitants could only gape in wonder, blinking in the blinding light that surrounded me. Those in charge had no choice. They immediately unlocked the chains that had for so long bound the prisoners.

As I turned once again to exit, the released prisoners, in a burst of energy and joy, swarmed out with me. Such jubilation had never been witnessed within these boundaries! I was eager to bring them back into the Kingdom.[120]

---

[120]   See Psalms 16:10 and Rev. 1:18

Reaching the surface didn't take long. The newly released beings eagerly flitted here and there, enjoying their new found freedom as I entered the tomb where my body had been laid.[121]

---

[121] Matt 27:60 See also Isa. 14:13-17

The sweet smell of myrrh and aloes permeated not only the tomb but the surrounding garden as well. These spices had soaked into the linen covering my body. Cold and lifeless, my corpse had been hastily wrapped in a long linen cloth along with the burial spices.

At the moment my spirit entered my body, the light radiating from the reunion slightly scorched the linen, creating a perfect photographic negative. This clue would be preserved; the Father had alerted certain believers to keep the relic safe for future generations.

The twelve-foot linen shroud showed my image, top to bottom, front to back. The cloth around my face also showed my facial features, front and back. Though photography hadn't yet been discovered by Earth's inhabitants, in time it would be. Many future generations would find faith because of my image on the cloth.

As I removed the shroud from my resurrected body, I carefully folded and placed it at one end of the tomb's burial bed.

"Good work." Michael greeted me. He and Gabriel were sitting on the other side, watching me as I folded the linen. They were smiling with joy as I readjusted my earthly body to my eternal self.

"Smells sweet," I noted as I laid the face cloth down.

"A bit overwhelming . . . You keeping the body?" Gabriel asked.

"Why not?" I beamed, still savoring the victory. "Sinless . . . It'll never deteriorate."

"The scars remain."

"Battle wounds. Will always remind me of Kingdom victory," I answered, still amazed and elated at knowing the job was completed. "I'm ready to return to my Father."

"Won't be long now." Gabriel said with a smile as he gave Michael a joyous high-five.

Leaving the tomb, I noticed the damage from the earthquake to the stone wall of the opening. Stooping to exit, I saw that the angels had already removed the stone by rolling it back up the slight incline. Smiling a "thank you" to them, they nodded, shrugging their shoulders. They were fully aware that my power now was far greater than theirs.

Two Roman soldiers, felled by my resurrection power, dazedly got up and ran out of the garden as fast as they could. Left on the ground was the broken Roman seal.

Exiting behind me, the angels tussled playfully in the garden before re-entering. I could tell they were excited, and I was too! Though I'd been through an ordeal, the thrill of victory for the Kingdom was extremely energizing.

Standing unnoticed just outside the tomb, I watched in interest as Mary Magdalene came with a basket of spices to finish the job Joseph had started. As she approached, she noticed the stone had already been removed from the door. She quickly left and soon afterward Peter and John ran into the garden.[122]

As she approached, she noticed the stone had already been removed from the door. She quickly left and soon afterward Peter and John ran into the garden. John, being

---

[122] The counselor Joseph of Arimathea begged Pilate for the body of Jesus and laid him in his own tomb. See John 19:38.

younger, reached the entrance first, but it was bold Peter who actually bent down to enter the tomb.

Noticing the linen with the photographic negative, Peter's eyes popped open in amazement. The image was enough to confirm the fact that I'd not only been wrapped in the grave clothes, but now was not in them.[123]

They left, too amazed to talk; but Mary, who had once again returned to the tomb, timorously stooped down to look inside. It was then she saw the two angels in white sitting, one at the head and the other at the foot where my body had lain. She began to sob.

"Why are you crying?" I asked gently

"Because they have taken away my Lord and I don't know where they've laid him." She turned around and saw me standing. She assumed I was the gardener.

"Sir, if you've moved him from here, show me and I'll take him away."

Even though she'd seen her brother Lazarus brought back from the dead, I realized she had not expected me to come back from such a death. My blood loss alone would have made my body incompatible with life.

"Mary." Her big brown eyes opened wide. "Master!"

"Don't touch me, for I've not yet ascended to my Father. But go to my brothers and tell them that I'm going to my Father and your Father and to my God and your God."

This message would be repeated until the whole earth would be aware of the meaning: Lucifer's previous authority over them was now legally and officially terminated. THE WORD offered life; those who believed in me could enter the Kingdom of God as adopted sons. It wasn't a list of rules and rituals that made Heaven possible for mankind, but

---

[123] John 20:4-8 When John saw the cloths, he believed.

the love a Father had for those who were lost and sitting in darkness.

The next forty days the news of my resurrection spread like wildfire all through Jerusalem and into the outlying provinces. The truth would never be quenched; the sacrifice would never be outdated.

My job on Earth was finished.

Returning to the Father was a joyful experience. Running into the inner chamber, I embraced him as he embraced me.

"It's finished; we've won the victory."

"Now we must win the war."

With a couple thousand years of earth time left, our job was to empower each of Earth's believers with our Spirit in order to strengthen them to withstand Lucifer's many attacks. Lies were still rampant, and the unwary believed them. But the words of truth had been spoken, the light had been shone, and never again would the world wait in darkness.

From Heaven I saw the Father send His Spirit to Earth in a magnificent way. A shimmering cloud descended upon the earth. Rising high into the atmosphere it took on a form consisting of every soul on Earth who believed in me. Toes, feet, hands—every cell of this body contained a vital part. The redeemed were all part of its body; the Holy Spirit was in them, and they were in Him.[124]

Every believer down through the ages became a part of this magnificent cloud. From the head, each cell received orders and each cell obeyed. A mighty force to be reckoned with, the forces of evil would never be strong enough to defeat it.

Complete restoration of all things would happen; it was only a matter of time.

---

[124]   John 14:20

Chapter 25

Exiting the Archives

I will ransom them from the power of the grave; I will redeem them from death:

Hosea 13:14

Jeric glanced up, enlightenment in his eyes; "It was the Two-Edged Sword! THE WORD was so sharp it could discern the thoughts and intents of the heart. Unlike Adam, Jesus was not deceivable.

So you found the answer to your question? asked Korel.

"Yes. The Word of God was what defeated evil. Jesus, with the anointing of the Father, was the embodiment of THE WORD.[125] Neither Satan with his tricks nor the Pharisees with their evil intents could defeat him.

"We're clean because of the words he spoke to us."[126] Korel added.

"Why go any further?" Jano interjected. "The greatest event in human history is HIS victory over sin and death."

"Fun event to watch!"

"Want to see it again?"

---

125 John 10:36
126 John 15:3

The friends looked at each other, grinning at the prospect of viewing it a second time.

"Let's do it."

"I'm game."

"Rewind."

The instant Jesus arose from the dead was the most electrifying moment. Backing the archives to the spot, the group settled back to experience it again.

Only seconds into the replay, Korle caught sight of a figure they hadn't noticed before.

"Wait! See the seraph? Isn't that Jucola?" All their attention had earlier been focused on the massive exodus from the Pit. Now they saw that among the crowd was the tall doorkeeper.

Yes! As a released prisoner of war he now was exiting with the others.

The archive room erupted into cheers. Jucola's earlier story had not included this ending, leaving them somewhat curious.

Following Jucola to the surface, they observed him glancing here and there as he refocused his eyes to the beauty of trees, grass, and living, healthy beings. To say he was elated was a complete understatement.

The normally motionless angel, newly reborn into life was dancing and shouting for joy. He ran through the fields and splashed in the water, totally unseen by the humans on Earth. Eventually he happily boarded a waiting Skyper and returned to his heavenly home.

The story of Jesus had impacted the friends with unrestricted merriment. They danced happily as they witnessed once more the resurrection of the Savior of the world. Jesus had conquered death; they would never forget his gift.

Chapter 26

Adventures in Heaven Await Us

In the resurrection they . . . are as the angels of God.
Mat 22:30

The celebrations in the Highest Heaven were thrilling! Jesus, seated at the right hand of the Father welcomed them all back with words of love, appreciation and affection.

In Heaven there's no sickness, disease, cheaters, nor liars. All previous sins were forgiven, and as the eras sped by in rapid succession, the trials and experiences of Earth were forgotten by its former inhabitants.

Together again on the eighth heavenly day after creation, the sons settled into a glorious pattern where all worked together and flourished. The adventures of LIFE were many, and inexhaustible.

Jano and Korel met on a regular basis for horseback riding, skydiving, baseball games and other fun sports. Korel's passion of creating new strains of apples retained its fascination for him; he invited Jano to join him in his experimentation and discoveries. Jano readily accepted the invitation.

The Sons of God, many more by this time as all of the Redeemed had become joint heirs with their Savior, enjoyed creating new stars and planets. Shouting for joy at the completion of each new realm, the heavens continually rang out with delighted laughter.[127]

Guardian angels were re-assigned back to their original jobs, though this past temporary diversion of work had left a long-lasting impression on them. Forever friends, these angels would still never understand redemption in the same way as would those who'd escaped from the addictions of evil.

Meanwhile Korel, gone from his orchards and gardens for over a thousand years, was eager to return to them; the joy of gardening still held a strong interest for him.

"Ziphotan, here we come!" he exclaimed to Jano and anyone else within earshot. Jano, who now also resided on Ziphotan was just as eager to return. The angelic friends once more boarded a Skyper and headed to their homes.

Korel and Jano along with their friends were satisfied, knowing those intended for salvation had all been redeemed. They, along with Jesus, would not need to worry about the sons of perdition who preferred evil over good. These lost ones had chosen their fate, and the choice had been their own.[128] Peace had been restored; all was well for eternity.

As they made the journey toward their homes the two friends planned to visit the archives again, but at this point that visit has never happened. Too many exciting adventures in Heaven have prevented their return. Maybe later . . . .

---

[127] See Gal 4:4-7 and Eph 1:4-5
[128] John 17:12

Chapter 27

Epilogue

I have waited for your salvation, O Lord.

Gen. 49:18

Millions of light years away deep in a black hole existed the antichrist Lucifer, the false prophet and all liars.

Who's to say? Millions of years, millions and millions of eternities, some time way out in the future when eons of eras have passed and no one remembers anything about the days of "mankind," somewhere, perhaps, a repentant Pinnac and others like him will find the miracle of THE REDEMPTION, paid by Jesus for all time and eternity.

In an eternal world with a LOVING HEAVENLY FATHER, all things are possible.[129]—Even the conversion and restoration of the most evil one who caused the banishment of one-third of the angels?[130] That question can only be answered by THE WORD and ETERNAL FATHER OF LIGHT.[131]

---

[129]   Nothing is impossible with God. Luke 1:37
[130]   See Matt 18:11-13. Even just one lost sheep causes the Shepherd to leave the rest to look for it. Also note Heb 6:4-6 for the likelihood of repentance from those in question.
[131]   James 1:17

The story of sin and its forgiveness should never be forgotten. Jesus, willing to pay the ultimate price made a way for all to return to the loving Father; all can find themselves once again reunited with HIM.

Though the story of Jesus can never be completely told, in reading this trilogy one can experience the truths of the Gospel while imagining wonderful adventures in an eternal world. May all who read the words written in these books find the Savior, and in knowing HIM, discover true joy and happiness.

The way has been paid for all to return to the Father. Why not do it today?

If you open the door, I'll come in. Rev. 3:20

About the Twinkling Series . . .

When I was a young mother up on the farm, I would listen to the Christian radio station as I went about my work. My favorite program was from 8-8:30 every night with Kathryn Kuhlman. She was an early charismatic preacher known primarily for the spontaneous healings that took place during her services.

One night she spoke about the formation of the earth, fallen angels and the creation of man. I was fascinated, as I'd never before heard such in-depth explanations. The desire to write a story on the subject was birthed in my heart and grew year by year. Reading the scriptures throughout the following 35 years with her teaching in mind continually verified the truth of her words.

One Sunday in 2007 our church music minister announced she had a word from the Lord for someone —highly unusual in our denomination. After church she approached me. "Marilyn, I saw this vision so plainly. I saw a feather pen, paper, and ink. I believe you are to write." Her eyes were misty as she imparted these words.

"Perhaps this is an encouragement to finish the musical I'm working on," I replied.

"It's something different, but you'll have to confirm this yourself. Has God been speaking to you about anything else?"

Yes, he had.

Thus was born the trilogy: THE TWINKLING © 2008, Dark Stars of THE TWILIGHT © 2009 and TWICE SHARPENED, The Two-Edged Sword © 2010. Marilyn Olson